LONE HAND

Cole McCabe had a price on his head, but Chief Detective Frank Holbrooke gave him a chance to redeem himself by ridding the western trails of the badmen and robbers preying on Wells Fargo coaches. Not discouraged by the odds against him, McCabe proved an implacable and unrelenting foe to the badmen. But there were to be complications and setbacks which would not be resolved until the final, bitter shootout. Could he survive?

Books by Corba Sunman
in the Linford Western Library:

RANGE WOLVES

CORBA SUNMAN

LONE HAND

Complete and Unabridged

LINFORD
Leicester

First published in Great Britain in 2000 by
Robert Hale Limited
London

First Linford Edition
published 2001
by arrangement with
Robert Hale Limited
London

British Library CIP Data

Sunman, Corba
Lone hand.—Large print ed.—
Linford western library
1. Western stories
2. Large type books
I. Title
823.9′14 [F]

ISBN 0–7089–5965–2

Published by
F. A. Thorpe (Publishing)
Anstey, Leicestershire

Set by Words & Graphics Ltd.
Anstey, Leicestershire
Printed and bound in Great Britain by
T. J. International Ltd., Padstow, Cornwall

This book is printed on acid-free paper

1

Cole McCabe eased his tired horse as it staggered on the long upward slope and threw a glance over his wide shoulder for signs of pursuit. It had been just his luck to cross trails with a bunch of rustlers being chased by a posse and have some of the lawmen figure him for one of the gang cutting away from the main party. Three hard-riding, straight-shooting possemen had seen his trail and latched on to him, chasing him for miles and twice getting into gunshot range before his bay finally outran them.

He reined in and stepped down from his high saddle, a tall, powerful man in his middle-twenties. Dressed in a dusty blue store suit, he wore a sun-faded black Stetson low over his dark eyes. His weathered face was rugged, darkened to the colour of old saddle leather by the intense sunlight of the illimitable western ranges. His nose was slightly out of line, having been broken twice. A bushy, untrimmed moustache concealed the firmness of his mouth, and the tenacious line of his jaw exhibited the confidence and obstinacy of his nature.

Around his lean waist was buckled a black cartridge belt, its cutaway holster, containing a .45 Colt revolver, thonged to his right thigh. His dark eyes were narrowed against the glare of the westering sun, and he squinted for long minutes at the haze on his back trail. Then he relaxed, for there was no longer any sign of pursuit. The lawmen had finally given up on him. Perhaps their horses were tired when they first spotted him. His agile mind raked over the situation. Whatever the reason for their disappearance, he was relieved to escape the inevitability of being run to earth and forced to reveal his identity and intentions, for the success of his work depended on secrecy and anonymity.

He led the bay up the slope and crossed the skyline, then loosened the saddle girth and trailed his reins, permitting the horse to rest and graze. Drawing his Winchester .45–40 from its saddleboot, he went back to the skyline and hunkered down to watch patiently for the possemen. But his back trail was silent and still, the limitless range brooding in the waning light of the passing day. The only movement anywhere in that vast stillness was the black speck of a buzzard hovering far above in the limitless vault of the sky.

He began to relax as the minutes passed with no further sign of pursuit, but his alertness remained at a high peak from his long experience of riding the back trails. He could not afford to act like an ordinary man. From the age of fourteen, when his parents were murdered, he had been forced by circumstance to follow a trail that led him eventually into the life of a gunman with a low price on his head.

In those early days he had been just a reckless kid who reared himself by using his wits and concentrating on the wrong tenets of life. He had realized from the death of his parents that in this savage world a man needed to be able to defend himself. He had trailed the two killers responsible for his predicament and rid the world of their brutal, useless lives, although by so doing he had unwittingly placed himself outside the law that had failed his parents and then demanded his life for doing its work. But he had fled into the great wilderness of Arizona and New Mexico, concentrating on gaining top skill with a gun while drifting deeper and deeper into the dark maze that was the life and way of a gunslinger.

He had made a living by hiring out his guns to anyone who needed protection or required force to be brought against any individuals who would not toe the line. But he had never committed murder, although the reputation he gained through the ensuing years made no distinction in that area. Neither had he stolen. His mother's strict influence on the first fourteen years of his life had remained long after her death, although there were times when he figured that his subsequent actions must have made her turn over in her grave on a number of occasions.

He had disliked the reality of his life. Having a price on his head was a handicap which was impossible to overcome. No matter where he went, there was always someone to point a finger at him, or whisper his name and denounce him to the law. He had accustomed himself to riding the back trails and shunning the company of his fellow men. He took gun jobs, and usually the mere threat of his ever-growing reputation was sufficient to cow the opposition. He never drew first and had never been bested for speed and accuracy. But he was aware that his life was limited by his reputation, for it was inevitable that some day, if he did not forsake his present way of life, he would meet the man who was fated to be his master and spend the rest of eternity on some lonely Boot Hill.

But all that had been in the days before he came up against Frank Holbrooke, the chief detective in the south-east for Wells Fargo. His life had changed when he took Holbrooke's advice to get back on the straight and narrow by joining Wells Fargo as a trouble shooter. Holbrooke had promised to get him a pardon if he proved that he was reformed and amenable to the rule of law, which he had done over a period of two years, operating in Kansas and Colorado against the badmen who thought Wells Fargo was an easy touch where robbery was concerned.

Now he was looking forward to getting that promised pardon, planning to quit Wells Fargo and settle down to cattle ranching. But first he had to smash the Sam Gotch gang, which was operating in the area around Dodge City and Abilene, Kansas. Three westbound coaches had been hit in the past month, and Holbrooke had given McCabe the job of redressing the situation . . .

Darkness came before he moved from his position, and he was now certain that the possemen had given up. His life, since his rehabilitation, had been complicated by lawmen who were unaware of his reformed character, for he was working undercover, relying on his reputation to get in with the lawless element who were opposed to any kind of order. His hatred of killers was like a fire burning inside him.

He eased back from the ridge and went down to the bay, which was rested and impatient to be on the trail again. Tightening the cinch, he swung into the saddle and rode on, heading north-west across the undulating plain of Kansas. He had been resting up in Coffeeville after a running battle with three outlaws who had robbed the Wells Fargo stage near Baxter Springs when Holbrooke contacted him with information about the notorious Sam Gotch, an unscrupulous outlaw whose run of lawlessness spanned more than two decades of robbery and murder.

Using the stars to maintain his direction, he was intent upon reaching a spot ten miles south of the cowtown of Hickory, where the stage line branched from the Santa Fe trail to make its run to Dodge City. He knew the spot well, and had to reach it before the planned robbery was due to take place. Around midnight he made cold camp, and knee-hobbled his bay before rolling himself in his blankets. He slept like a wild animal, ready to spring up in defence at the slightest suspicious noise. When the sun rose to warm the ground he awoke, ate a frugal breakfast, then broke camp.

He rode on, and for two days traversed a silent, brooding land of grass, seeing no other traveller in the unchanging scenery that was tortured by dancing heat waves. On the third day, around noon, he paused on a skyline and looked down a long, undulating slope to see twin wheel tracks in the middle distance snaking through the lower ground roughly one hundred yards ahead.

A long sigh escaped McCabe as he reined up in cover and looked around, checking that he was in the right spot. He took a letter from his pocket and read it, although the information contained in it was burned into his memory. He nodded slowly. This was the spot. He did not question how Holbrooke gained his information about the planned raid. The chief detective had his own methods of learning what the lawless men in his area were planning, and he had been right too many times in the last two years for McCabe to have any doubt about the veracity of his information.

Satisfied that he had reached the right spot, he sought cover where he could overlook a stand of cottonwoods situated at the top of a rise in the trail. He had two hours to wait for the stage to reach the rise, and at some time in that period the Sam Gotch gang was due to ride into the cottonwoods with the intention of lying in wait for the coach.

McCabe backed his horse off the skyline and slid from his saddle, his right hand instinctively snaking his Winchester out of its boot. He took a pair of field glasses from his saddlebag and hunkered down to check out the entire area. Satisfied that the robbers were not yet approaching, he relaxed and ate cold food, then slaked his thirst with brackish water from his canteen.

He looked at the wanted posters Holbrooke had sent him. There were five men in the Gotch gang. Sam Gotch was a tall, bulky man who was inordinately strong. In his early forties, he had a vivid white knife scar down the left side of his face. His eyes were filled with inherent brutality, which he had displayed often in his violent career. Then there was Rattlesnake Riley, a tall, thin individual, who wore a snakeskin hatband on his Stetson. The other three men of the gang, Wiley Benns, George Tropman and Asa Pyle, were not described on the posters.

McCabe sat considering the coming action as the long minutes passed. He moved his horse farther back from the ridge, knee-hobbled the animal, then dropped to the ground and crawled forward until he could again study the stand of trees. His slitted blue eyes narrowed even more when, using his glasses, he picked out the figures of five men standing together under the trees, their horses cropping the lush grass underfoot. They had arrived silently and unseen.

Three of the men had rough gunny-sack masks covering their faces, and McCabe looked left and right along the trail. He spotted a banner of dust rising in the air to the east and watched

11

its approach until he could make out the details of the swaying Concord coach that was approaching. The six-horse team was moving tirelessly at a concerted gallop, their necks outstretched, hooves pounding as they threw their weight into their collars and hauled the heavy coach along the rough trail. The driver was leaning forward in his high seat, urging the horses to greater effort, and a shotgun guard was clinging desperately to the side-rail of his seat as the dust-ridden vehicle lurched and rolled like a ship at sea in a high gale. The rumble of the wheels, the eternal cracking of the driver's whip and the pounding hooves came easily to his ears.

Using his field glasses, McCabe saw the five waiting outlaws tighten their cinches and swing into their saddles. He picked out the leading figure and studied Gotch's brutal face, noting the knife scar that ran from the top of the left ear down across the cheek to the side of the mouth. He nodded soberly, aware that there was no chance of mistaking Sam Gotch.

McCabe jacked a cartridge into the breech of his Winchester and eased into a more comfortable position on the skyline. The riders moved out of cover and positioned themselves in a spaced line across the narrow trail, sunlight glinting on their drawn pistols.

There was an immediate reaction from the two men on the high seat of the rapidly approaching coach. The driver stood up and hauled back on his reins while the guard snatched up the double-barrelled shotgun that was leaning at his side, throwing it upwards and forward into the aim. One of the five riders lifted his drawn sixgun, and McCabe, already squinting through his gunsight, instantly squeezed his trigger.

The flat crack of the shot threw a string of echoes across the silent plain. The rifle jerked in McCabe's hands and the robber aiming at the shotgun guard stiffened under the impact of the speeding slug. He pitched sideways out of his saddle, and instant pandemonium broke out among the remaining four robbers as the echoes of the shot reverberated sullenly away to the horizon. They spurred their mounts desperately, galloping off in different directions, quickly fleeing the scene, the robbery instantly forgotten.

McCabe threw lead after them and saw one jerk under the bite of a speeding slug. The man swayed in his saddle but retained his seat, and soon vanished over the nearest skyline. The others drew out of range and kept going. McCabe heaved a sigh and watched the coach slowing to a halt. When it had stopped he got to his feet and swung into his saddle to ride down the slope, thrusting his rifle into its saddleboot as he did so.

The shotgun guard covered McCabe as he approached, the twin muzzles of his fearsome weapon gaping menacingly. The driver had dismounted from his high seat and was standing by the fallen robber, who was lying on his back, arms outflung, a dull patch of blood on his shirtfront. A frightened female face peered at McCabe from the window of the coach as he reined in and leaned forward in his saddle.

The driver came to McCabe's side, shaking his head in wonder. He was short and bandy-legged, his wrinkled, bronzed face covered with a sheen of sweat and dust. A sixgun was holstered in a sagging gun-belt buckled around his waist. He pushed back his Stetson and wiped his forehead on his right sleeve.

'You sure was handy, mister,' he observed, his pale blue eyes glinting. 'And you've put an end to that robber's business. He's drilled plumb centre. It's the first time one of Sam Gotch's bunch has been made to pay for his crimes.'

'He was about to shoot the guard,' McCabe said. 'I tried for a wing shot but there wasn't much time.'

'It's better to kill his kind in cold blood.' The driver held out a gnarled hand. 'I'm beholden to you, pardner. I'm Eli Benson and my guard is Chuck Denny. Are you figuring on visiting Hickory? It's a one-horse town about ten miles from here. That's where we're headed, and I'd sure admire to buy you a drink.'

'I figure to be around Hickory for a spell.' McCabe's dark eyes narrowed as he considered the nature of his business. 'You looked at the robber. Do you recognize him?'

'I've seen him around town more than once.' Benson shook his head. 'That gunny-sack mask he was wearing ties him in with the Sam Gotch bunch that's been raising hell around here for weeks now. We'll tote him into town and drop him off on the sheriff's doorstep. Josh Sarran has long been out've luck looking for Gotch and his pards.'

McCabe glanced around. The range was deserted now, but he figured the robbers could be waiting in cover for him to ride off before returning to resume their interrupted business.

'I'll ride into town with you,' he decided.

'Be glad of your company,' Benson replied.

The dead robber was wrapped in a slicker and lifted to the roof of the coach and tied in place. McCabe hitched his bay to the rear of the coach, climbed inside the vehicle, and gazed at the young woman who was the only occupant. She was staring at him in a state of shock, as if fearing that he would turn out to be a robber.

She was, he decided, the most beautiful female he had ever seen, despite the fact that she was looking uncomfortable in the stifling atmosphere of the coach. Her blue dress was covered in a thin mantle of dust, and she was holding a handkerchief with which she occasionally dabbed at her face and forehead. She returned his gaze with interest, her blue eyes filled with curiosity, her lips slowly stretching into a smile as she realized that he was not one of the hold-up men. Her long blond hair fell about her slim shoulders in a golden cascade.

'I'm Rana Harpley,' she said, lurching sideways as the coach started forward. 'It was lucky for us you were on the spot when those robbers appeared, and quite courageous of you to tackle them. My father is Willard Harpley. He runs the Wells Fargo office in Hickory. He'll be pleased to meet you, I'm sure.'

McCabe shook his head. 'It was easy to put those crooks off balance,' he said. 'They were keyed up to hit the coach, and when I poked my nose in they were throwed considerable. At that moment they didn't know if a posse had caught up with them. Their kind don't take chances, so they pulled out, just in case.'

'And you're riding with us now in case they show up again.' She nodded approval, dabbing at her forehead and cheeks with the already moist handkerchief.

'I'm heading for Hickory,' he admitted,

'and riding the coach makes a pleasant change to sitting a saddle.'

'I didn't get your name.' Her blue eyes were narrowed against the glare of the sun at the window. She was grasping the leather strap at her shoulder, which prevented her from being hurled around by the jolting, bouncing movements of the coach as it was hauled westward over the ungraded road. McCabe felt a tremor of interest filter into his chest.

'Call me Cole.' He refrained from giving his full name in case she had heard of him.

'Is that your given name or your family name?'

He smiled. 'It's the only one I got.'

A faint frown settled on her forehead and the smile faded from her lips. McCabe heaved a silent sigh and braced himself in the opposite corner, allowing his body to sway with the movements of the lurching vehicle. He was searching his mind for something to say when a gun crashed and a bullet

19

bored through the rear of the coach, missing his head by an inch or two. He ducked instinctively and drew his Colt with a slick motion.

'Get down on the floor,' he rapped, and the girl obeyed instantly, flinging herself down, her face betraying fear as she looked up at him.

McCabe slid sideways, opened the window and peered out at their back trail. His expression hardened when he saw four riders hammering along the trail in their dust, gunsmoke spurting about them as they fired at the coach. Overhead, the crack of a rifle spanged flatly, and then the crash of a pistol indicated that both the guard and the driver on the high seat of the vehicle were buying into the fight.

Cocking his gun, McCabe leaned out of the window and opened fire at the pursuing riders. He fired three shots in rapid succession, and compressed his lips when the nearest rider reared backwards in his saddle then pitched sideways and fell to the ground. The outlaw hit the hard trail with a thump and bounced a couple of times before lying motionless, his gun discarded and his arms outflung.

Bullets from the pursuers thudded into the back of the coach and McCabe winced as a lightning pain flashed across the top of his right shoulder. He ducked inside the coach to check himself, and was surprised to find the cloth of his shirt torn. Blood was soaking into the thin fabric. But it was a flesh wound and did not inconvenience him. He glanced at the girl cowering on the floor, tightened his grip on his gun and leaned out the window again to resume the fight.

The guard and the driver were firing rapidly at the pursuing riders, their hot lead compelling the robbers to drop back. The coach continued at a reckless pace, swaying and jolting over the rough ground. McCabe drew a bead on the nearest rider, ignoring the bullets crackling around him. He fired, but saw no visible result of the shot. The coach was lurching from side to side and he tried to allow for the movement. He fired again, and the rider suddenly slumped in his saddle but did not fall.

The three riders immediately reined away. McCabe heaved a sigh and started to reload his gun from the loops on his cartridge belt. The girl got up from the floor. Her face was flushed as she sat back in her seat.

'Have they given up?' she demanded, and added, when he nodded, 'I guess we're getting too close to town for them.'

'Is there much crookedness around here?' he asked, and she nodded emphatically.

'I'll say! Did you notice the masks some of the robbers were wearing? That bunch is called the gunny-sack gang, and they've stopped this coach three times in the past month, killing two guards in the process. They also hit the bank over in Juniper Creek, and they're rustling out on the range.'

'Sounds like they're on overtime,' McCabe observed. 'What's the local law doing about it?'

'Sheriff Sarran is a good man, but he doesn't get much help. My father is about the only man who supports the law in this county, and he says it's an uphill job. He figures the only way to beat these badmen is to play them at their own game. He's told the sheriff that he'll bring in some gunslingers to help fight the trouble, but the sheriff won't hear of it. He figures he can handle it if his luck changes.'

'Gunslingers might not be the answer.' McCabe shrugged. 'They can become a worse problem than the badmen themselves.'

'That's what the sheriff says.' She paused, her blue eyes narrowed as she looked McCabe over. 'Do you have business in the county or are you just riding through?'

'I got some business to attend to.'

He smiled. 'Your father is Willard Harpley, huh?'

'Sure.' Her eyes narrowed and became filled with curiosity. 'Do you know him?'

'I'm one of the gunslingers your father threatened to bring in. Frank Holbrooke sent me.'

Her face changed expression instantly and she suppressed a sigh. 'Gunslingers are a necessary evil, my mother says. She's in favour of fighting fire with fire. But is there only one of you? One man can't handle Gotch's bunch, no matter how good he is.'

'There's only one gang so Frank Holbrooke sent me.' McCabe peered out the window and checked their surroundings. There was no longer any sign of the robbers.

'There's trouble on the range in addition to the outlaws,' the girl went on. 'Joel Slater has been talking about fencing in Mulejaw Creek, where Wells Fargo has a way-station and need the water for its stock. Pa takes that kind of talk seriously. The creek doesn't belong to Slater and he has no rights there.'

'Do you figure your father is wrong, wanting to bring in hired guns to keep the water flowing?'

'Not if it keeps men like Slater from breaking the law.'

'So we'll be on the same side of the fence.' He smiled.

'As long as you stay on the right side of the law,' she countered, firming her lips. 'You said that some gunslingers turn out to be worse than the badmen they fight.'

He nodded gravely. 'I'm a regular detective employed by Wells Fargo,' he admitted. 'Frank Holbrooke is my boss.'

'I know Mr Holbrooke well.' Relief showed in her dusty features. 'If he employs you then you must be all right.'

'I'm glad to know that.' McCabe grinned. He finished reloading the spent chambers of his gun and holstered the big weapon. Then he relaxed in his corner and studied the girl's beautiful face, aware that his stay in this district of the Wells Fargo network could prove to be very interesting.

2

The Kansan cowtown of Hickory occupied a level stretch of ground near a wide creek, and consisted of two rutted streets in the shape of a cross. The main street ran east to west along the trail into and out of town, and along it were huddled, on either side, the various places of business forming the nucleus of the small community. Most of the buildings were of clap-board, and a number were single storey with wooden facades to create the illusion of height. The livery barn was at the eastern end of town, standing apart from the remainder of the buildings, with a corral out back and a water trough by the front wall of the barn. North and South Streets contained the majority of the dwellings of the community.

McCabe peered from the window of

the coach as it rattled along the wide street. He saw the Wells Fargo office, its big sign prominently displaying the names of the two men who had founded the largest network of transport and communication in the entire continent. There was a big hotel, one saloon, a general store and a brick-built bank. He saw a large sign over another brick building proclaiming that it was the office and jail of the county sheriff, and the coach shuddered to a halt in front of it.

McCabe alighted quickly and turned to hold out a hand to the girl, who smiled at him as she accepted his offer. The top of her blond head was barely level with his broad shoulder, he noted, when she stood beside him, and the light touch of her hand in his started a thread of unaccustomed emotion unravelling in his breast which he quickly smothered.

'You'll be wanting to talk to my father,' she suggested, and he shook his head.

'Your father doesn't know me or why I'm here,' he said. 'I'm in the area under cover, and I told you in strict confidence that I'm working for Wells Fargo to rest your mind about me.'

'The fact that you stopped the coach robbery was enough to set my mind at rest about you.' She smiled. 'Don't worry. Your secret will be safe with me. I hope to see you around town, Cole. Perhaps you'll come and have supper with us sometime?'

'Thanks for the offer, but I have a feeling I'll be busy from here on in.' He touched his hat to her as the driver appeared with a large bag, which he dropped at the girl's feet.

'Here you are, Rana,' Benson said. 'I hope you weren't too scared by the hold-up.'

'It would have been much worse if Cole hadn't been on hand.' She smiled at McCabe as she picked up her bag. 'I hope you'll look me up before you leave town.' Her voice was low-pitched and friendly. 'I live in the big, white-painted house on North Street, the second on the right.'

'I'll surely do that.' McCabe smiled.

The girl turned and departed. Eli Benson lifted his hat and scratched his thick shock of grey hair as he gazed after her. He shook his head slowly, a big grin on his rugged face as he looked at McCabe. He slapped dust from his jacket and hitched up the sagging gun-belt around his ample middle.

'You sure made a big impression on that gal,' he observed. 'But we better report to the law office. Mebbe now the sheriff will get a line on the rest of those robbers.'

McCabe glanced towards the law office and saw two men in the act of emerging from it. One was squat and grizzled, probably in his fifties. He was wearing dark pants and a white shirt on which was glinting a six-pointed sheriff's star. His feet were encased in a pair of highly polished riding-boots. A gun-belt encircled his thick waist, containing a pearl-handled sixgun nestling in a low-slung holster on his right thigh. The man accompanying the sheriff was tall and raw-boned, and walked with a swaggering gait, his fleshy face set in what seemed to be a permanent scowl. He wore two guns on crossed cartridge belts, and looked as if he knew how to use them.

'Here's Josh Sarran now,' said Benson.

'Who's the guy with him?' McCabe asked.

'Joel Slater. Owns the JS ranch fifteen miles south of town. Slater is a hard man.' Benson glanced at McCabe's harsh face. 'I don't reckon he's in your class though. What you did to Gotch and his gang was somethin' else.'

McCabe shrugged, and stood motionless and silent while the coach driver gave the sheriff an account of what had happened at the hold-up. Sarran eyed McCabe as the story unfolded, his face surprisingly unwrinkled despite his apparent years, and evinced no surprise as the exciting news was imparted to him, although his eyes were narrowed and glinting.

'That was good work, McCabe,' he said when Benson fell silent. 'I had a cable from Frank Holbrooke telling me about you. Frank is a man who never exaggerates, and he praised you. But you sure made a big start against Gotch. Was it luck, or the way you normally work?'

'I guess I was in the right spot at the right time,' McCabe responded, wondering why Holbrooke had exposed him.

Sarran nodded. He waved an impatient hand. 'Get that body off'n the top of the coach, Eli. I wanta look at it. Ain't Sam Gotch hisself, is it, McCabe?'

'Nope. But I recognized Gotch in the bunch before the coach was held up,' McCabe replied.

The sheriff glanced frowningly at him. 'You ever met Gotch?'

'No. I got a wanted poster with his picture on it.'

'Pity you didn't kill Gotch when he was under your gun,' Joel Slater's voice was harsh and low-pitched. His blue eyes blazed with inner fire when McCabe met his gaze.

'The guy I shot was drawing a bead on the guard,' McCabe said. 'I figured to prevent bloodshed. But don't worry about Gotch. I'll get out after him soon as my horse is rested.'

'Pretty confident, ain't yuh?' Slater shook his head. 'In my book, talk is cheap.'

'McCabe's got a right to talk any way he wants,' Eli Benson snapped, and it was plain that the coach driver did not like Slater. 'You should have seen the way he let into that bunch of no-goods. He sent them running like the tails of their hosses were on fire. And when the bunch hit us again, from behind, he downed another and sent them running like they was in a hurry to reach the border. That gives him the right to talk any which-way.'

'What happened to the second robber

you downed?' Sarran demanded. 'Is he still out there on the trail?'

'Right where he dropped,' Benson rasped. 'My job was to get the coach safely into town. If you want the body you'll have to go out after it.'

'I'll be riding out later,' McCabe promised. 'I'll take care of the details.'

'You better come into my office and make an official report on what happened.' Sarran moved impatiently. 'I'll ride out with you when you're ready to leave. Gotch and his bunch have been running me and my posse ragged these past weeks. I need to take advantage of what you've done, McCabe.'

'I'd like the reason I'm here to be kept quiet.' McCabe spoke sombrely. 'It will make my job easier.'

'Sure. Anything you say.' Sarran nodded, grinning harshly. 'Just so long as we get results against the badmen. They've been giving me a hard time and I got a big score to settle with them. Hitting the bunch like you did will knock 'em flat-footed.'

Benson and Denny climbed on the coach and untied the body of the robber. McCabe helped the sheriff lower it to the ground, then stepped back. Sarran dropped to one knee and studied the face of the dead man for some moments before straightening.

'I ain't never seen him before,' he mused.

'I've seen him around town, and he's one of the Gotch gang,' Benson said. 'He was wearing a gunny-sack mask.'

'I'll go through my dodgers and see what I can turn up.' The sheriff looked around. A crowd of townsfolk had gathered on the sidewalk and Sarran beckoned to a short, fat man who was standing in the background. 'Ben, go fetch Hiram. He can get this guy ready for burial.'

The fat man nodded and departed unhurriedly. Benson slapped McCabe's thick shoulder.

'I'm hoping you'll have a drink with me later,' he said. 'You won't be able to buy anything in Grant's saloon while you're in town. It'll all be on me, pardner.'

'Thanks.' McCabe smiled. He met Joel Slater's hard gaze and the JS rancher shrugged his heavy shoulders and turned away.

'I got to be getting back to my place, Josh,' the rancher said to the sheriff. 'I'll see you when you get around to visiting, huh?'

'Sure thing. I'll be looking into that problem you mentioned and I'll let you know how it pans out.' The sheriff turned his attention to McCabe. 'Let's go to my office.' He looked into McCabe's eyes, his expression inscrutable, and McCabe wondered if he would get trouble from this particular lawman.

'I'll need you to look through my posters. You might be able to pin-point those of Gotch's gang who ain't been identified yet. Some of the buzzards could be living in town right under my nose and I wouldn't know them.'

'I'll take care of your horse, Cole,' Benson said. 'You'll be able to pick him up at the company barn when you want him.'

'Thanks. I'll book into the hotel while I'm in town.'

'I'll do that for you, and put your gear in your room,' Benson continued.

McCabe flashed the coach driver a grin, and Eli Benson shrugged and pulled a face. McCabe followed the sheriff to the law office, and dropped into a seat when the lawman sat down at his desk. Sarran opened a drawer, took out a stack of wanted posters, and held them out to McCabe.

'Run through them and see if you can pick out any of the crooks,' he suggested.

'It'll be a waste of time.' McCabe shrugged. 'Sam Gotch is known by sight and Rattlesnake Riley is easy to identify. Of the other two, one fell out of his saddle when I hit him, and I creased the other, so you can bet he'll stick close to Gotch.'

'Mebbe so.' Sarran took another poster out of his desk and showed it to McCabe. It was of McCabe himself, and the sheriff grinned harshly, his eyes gleaming. 'I guess you won't want this to be seen around town, huh? It could cause some confusion. A wanted gunnie out hunting outlaws and working hand in glove with the law.'

'You're right.' McCabe stifled a sigh. 'I've had to keep my past quiet, and most of the trouble I've had since working for Wells Fargo came from lawmen who didn't believe I'd turned over a new leaf.'

'You won't get any trouble from me.' Sarran returned McCabe's poster to his desk. 'I'll keep this locked up. Now let's get down to business. Holbrooke said I should go along with whatever you suggest. I must admit that I had my doubts about you, but here you are, turning up with one of Gotch's gang dead and another lying out on the trail. The last three coaches coming through here have been robbed by Gotch. He sure was making a name for hisself in this neck of the woods. But it looks like Holbrooke is right. You're gonna wipe out this gang without help.'

'Or die trying,' McCabe observed. 'I'd better get moving. You know what happened at the hold-up, and I'll be writing a report later. Right now I need to eat and rest up. I reckon you could send someone back along the trail to check on that other robber I downed. That won't wait until morning, and I'm not riding out until dawn.'

Sarran nodded. 'Consider it done. And you better watch your back around here. Gotch must have friends in town because he's always got top information about what's going on.'

'Thanks for the tip, but I got a habit of watching my back.' McCabe arose, his big figure bulking large in the office. He drew his pistol and checked the loads, then returned it to his holster. 'Be seeing you, Sheriff.' He touched a forefinger to his hatbrim. 'That'll be after I've scouted around the range and

checked out the tracks Gotch's bunch
left when they pulled out. They got to
be holed up someplace close by.'

'You're gonna be a mighty busy
man,' Sarran told him. 'I never found
tracks of Gotch, not since he started
riding around my county.'

McCabe left the office and paused
on the sidewalk to take a look around
the town. Evening was closing in. The
sun was low in the sky to the west, and
a faint breeze was blowing in from the
range. He saw Joel Slater riding along
the street, mounted on a black stallion
that seemed impatient to hit the trail.
There was still a crowd of townsfolk
standing around the stagecoach outside
the hotel, and he noted that his bay
had been taken from the back of the
vehicle. The horse was the main reason
why he was not riding out immediately.
The animal had been on the trail for
too long without good food and rest.

He saw a sign over a doorway
indicating the presence of a café, and
made for the establishment. He needed

hot food and coffee before sleep, and entered the café to find that it was busy. He sat down at a corner table and used his ears and eyes while waiting to be served. A flustered waitress finally came for his order, apologizing for keeping him waiting.

'I wouldn't want your job for a hundred dollars a week,' he said as she wrote down his order, and she flashed him a grateful smile, her hard expression relaxing somewhat. Her blue eyes shone momentarily, and McCabe suppressed a sigh as he wondered what was worrying her.

'That's considerate of you,' she replied. 'I admire your patience.' She glanced over her shoulder when someone called her, then excused herself and hurried away, lifting a hand to wipe a strand of blond hair off her heated forehead.

McCabe looked at the man in the doorway who had called the waitress. He was well dressed, wearing good-quality clothes — a brown store suit, white shirt and string tie. A flat-crowned plains hat was pulled tightly on his black head, and McCabe noted the harsh expression on the newcomer's thin features. The man's lips were pinched as if he was constantly holding a bad temper in check, and when the waitress reached him he grasped her left arm with such force that she uttered a cry of pain. She tried to pull away, but the man held her, his thin lips twisting with sadistic pleasure, his eyes gleaming angrily.

McCabe fought down a surge of anger and forced himself to remain seated. He could not hear what the man said, but the waitress shook her head and finally managed to wrench her arm free of his grasp, then hurried into the kitchen. The man stood gazing after her for a moment, then turned and bustled out the doorway, almost knocking over a youth who was entering. The youngster, aged about fifteen, fell back against the doorpost, and the bully half lifted his hand and shook his clenched fist under the youth's nose. The youngster ducked instinctively and came hurrying into the café. Looking around, he spotted McCabe and crossed to his table.

'Mr McCabe?' he queried, and McCabe nodded. 'I got a message for you. Mr Harpley, the Wells Fargo agent, would like to see you soon as you can make it. He says it's urgent. You got news come through from Frank Holbrooke, who's on his way to town.'

'Thanks. But it'll have to wait until I've eaten.' McCabe reached out a powerful hand and grasped the youth's sleeve as he turned to depart. 'Not so fast. I got some questions to ask. What's your name, and how come you're running errands for Wells Fargo?'

'I'm Billy Dean. I work for Wells Fargo.' A touch of pride sounded in the youth's voice. 'Some day I'm gonna be a driver like Eli Benson, and I wanta be as good with a gun as you are.'

McCabe smiled. 'I sure hope you make it, Billy. Tell me, who's the bully you ran into when you came in?'

Billy glanced towards the door and his expression hardened. 'That was Dave Thorn. He's a gambler in Grant's saloon. I can't wait till I'm full-growed so I can give him his come-uppance.'

'That's some ambition.' McCabe frowned at the degree of intensity displayed by the youngster. 'What's he done to you?'

'Among other things, he's been pestering my sister Rosie ever since he showed up around here.' Anger laced Billy's raw tone, and McCabe experienced a chill sensation in his chest. 'Rosie don't want nothing to do with Thorn, and my pa would have handled Thorn if he hadn't been shot in the back.'

'Killed?' McCabe compressed his lips. 'I'm sorry to hear that. How'd it happen?'

'Before I kill him, I'll make Thorn

tell me,' the youngster replied, his voice raw with anger.

The raw tone in Billy Dean's voice reminded McCabe of his own past, and he drew a sharp breath as a pang of emotion hit him hard. He was struggling to hold his feelings in check when the waitress emerged from the kitchen and came to the table with his order.

'Billy, what are you doing here?' she demanded.

'I brung a message for Mr McCabe. Wells Fargo business. Has Thorn been bothering you again, Rosie? He was leaving as I came in.'

'He don't bother me none.' The girl shook her blond head, but McCabe noted fear in her blue eyes. 'You better get back to Mr Harpley, Billy, and stay away from Thorn.'

'Tell Harpley I'll see him in about half an hour,' McCabe said, and Billy nodded and departed.

'I hope Billy wasn't bothering you,' Rosie said.

'Nope.' McCabe shook his head. 'He brought me a message. You got trouble with that Thorn feller?'

'No more than any other girl around here. He ain't a pleasant man, and won't take no for an answer.'

'Billy figures Thorn's responsible for your pa's death.'

'He told you that?' She frowned. 'He's never talked about it before.' She lifted her gaze to McCabe's set face.

'I'm a trouble shooter, and he's probably heard talk about me at the Wells Fargo office.' McCabe shook his head. 'What happened to your father? How did he die? And why does Billy think Thorn is responsible?'

She glanced around the crowded room, then shook her head. 'I'm trying to forget about that,' she said, 'and it wouldn't help to talk about it. I'd better get back to work. This is the rush hour and my boss'll grumble if I don't get a move on.'

'Sure. But I'm interested in any law-breaking goin' on around here so I'd

46

like to talk to you about your trouble. It could lead me to the people I'm interested in.'

'Are you a lawman?' Sudden hope flickered in her blue eyes but died quickly, and she shook her head and half turned away. 'It's better to leave the past buried,' she said sorrowfully. 'It'll be too painful to drag it all back. Dave Thorn set out to get our ranch and he had to kill my father to do it. He got away with murder and no one can make him pay for that. He squared himself with the law and it's over and done with.'

'Don't be too sure of that.' McCabe reached out and grasped her wrist and she looked down at him. 'Give me the facts and I'll check 'em out. Thorn sounds like a bad lot, and I'm interested in such men. What time do you get through? I'd like to know a little more about your trouble.'

'Give me an hour,' she replied reluctantly. 'But I'd rather not talk about it. We've had too much grief as it is.'

'I'll be waiting outside when you get done,' McCabe said firmly. 'You should take the trouble because Billy looks like he's primed to go off half-cocked at any time. You better think some about his attitude. He's festering inside, and could get himself killed.'

She sighed. 'All right.' Reluctance filled her tone but she seemed to take on a new resolve at the mention of her brother. 'But don't wait for me outside. I'll meet you at the Wells Fargo office.'

McCabe nodded and began to eat, and he was thoughtful as he watched the girl going about her business. By the time he had finished his meal the rush of custom in the café had been reduced to a trickle, and he paid and left, to find that night had fallen and the town was settling down. He looked around, his thoughts running unchecked. It was apparent that Sam Gotch had contacts in town, and if they were eliminated the outlaw would lose much of his power. But informants would have to be in a position to know about gold shipments and the like, and that kind of information was limited to Wells Fargo operatives, which could mean a leak in high places.

There was a frown of concentration on McCabe's face as he walked to the Wells Fargo office. Although he had been in this business for only two years he had quickly learned that there were patterns to this kind of lawlessness and if he found the key to this particular set-up he could clean up quickly. He needed to get a line on town life as soon as possible.

There were lights in the Wells Fargo office, and McCabe entered to find Billy Dean seated at the big desk. The youngster got to his feet when he saw McCabe, and the brooding expression on his face changed to one of pleasure.

'I'm holdin' the fort for Mr Harpley,' he said. 'He'll be back in a minute. He told me to ask you to wait for him.'

McCabe sat down on a corner of the desk. He noted that Billy was staring at his holstered sixgun, and drew the weapon and spun the cylinder.

'So you don't like Dave Thorn, huh?' he mused.

'You're dern tootin'! He killed my pa.'

'You got proof of that?'

'Nope. But no one else wanted Pa dead. Thorn put the squeeze on Pa, and when he couldn't buy the spread he turned snake, killed Pa and stole it.'

'Have you told this to anyone else?' McCabe frowned, aware that the boy could get on the wrong track for the rest of his life if he was not checked. 'You could get into trouble if it reached the wrong ears, Billy. How long has your pa been dead?'

'About a year, mebbe a little longer.' There was a hard glitter in Billy's pale eyes. 'I told the sheriff what I know but he wasn't interested. He warned me off — said I could go to jail for making false accusations.'

'I'm gonna talk to your sister shortly, and she'll give me the the low-down on what happened. I'll be looking for men around town who might be tied in with Sam Gotch and his bunch. If you got any idea who might be working in cahoots with the gang then I'll listen to you. But I don't want any wild accusations. If what you say about your father is true then I'll look into his death when I can get around to it. What makes you think Thorn is responsible?'

'He tried to get Pa to sell out. Pa wouldn't, and the next thing he was dead. After he was buried the lawyer, Art Pell, came to see Rosie and showed her a bill of sale which said Pa did sell out to Thorn. When Rosie refused to believe it, Pell took her to the bank and Ash Tolliver, the banker, showed her Pa's account, which had the money from the sale in it. It seems Pa was staying on to run the spread until Thorn wanted to take over.'

'And you figure your pa didn't sell out?'

'He never said a word about that, and knowing Pa, he would have told us if that had been in his mind.'

'So who is running the spread now?'

'A couple of hardcases moved in after the sheriff put us out. I been out there a couple of times, nosin' around, and I figure Newton and Harmer are using a wide loop. There's been rustling on the range since they moved in. There's a real crooked set-up been building up around here.'

A gun blasted somewhere along the street and McCabe lunged for the doorway. He reached the sidewalk as a riderless horse galloped by, stirrups flying, and then a spate of shots tore through the fading echoes, most of them slamming into the building where McCabe stood. McCabe hit the floor on his left shoulder, shouting for Billy to douse the light, and as darkness swooped in the raucous echoes of the shooting began to fade away.

3

McCabe ducked back into the office as Billy doused the lantern. Gun echoes were fading out there on the street and they were punctuated by a loud voice just outside the office demanding to know what was happening.

'That's Mr Harpley,' said Billy Dean. 'The shooting must be over.'

'Is there much gunplay around town?' McCabe asked.

'No. The sheriff keeps it down. Saturday nights are worst.'

'Light the lamp again.' McCabe narrowed his eyes as a match scraped and flared. He moved back from the doorway. His right hand was down on the butt of his gun as the door was opened.

A big man stepped across the threshold and entered the office. Lamplight threw harsh yellow glare around the room, and the newcomer paused, gazing at McCabe.

'Howdy?' he greeted. 'I reckon you'll be Cole McCabe. I'm Willard Harpley. My daughter told me how you saved the stagecoach. I know about your past. It's about time Holbrooke did something about Sam Gotch.' He held out a big hand and McCabe stepped forward to grasp it. Harpley was wide-shouldered, his blue eyes narrowed and gleaming. A blond moustache covered his top lip, and McCabe could see where Rana Harpley got her looks from. Harpley was dressed in a brown store suit, and a holstered sixgun was buckled around his waist. He seemed to be man enough for the important job he was doing, exuding an air of confidence and determination.

'Holbrooke is coming. here, ain't he?' McCabe said. 'Maybe he's gonna run this thing personal. I've only been working for him a couple of years. Maybe he ain't got faith in me yet.'

'That ain't the case. Holbrooke gave

you a big build-up, and when Frank talks like that he'll stay out of it and let you get to work. And you've made a good start. If you can make hay outa that fact then Gotch don;t stand a chance.'

'What was the shooting outside?'

'I didn't get the rights of it. I saw a riderless horse running along the street right after the shots were fired at the east end of town. I ducked into an alley, and before I could get here a whole mess of shooting broke out.'

'Most of which struck the front of this office. McCabe spoke grimly. 'I figger it was meant for me. That shooting along the street was likely done to draw me outside. I'd better get out there and see what's doing.'

'I wanted to talk to you about the way you plan to handle Gotch and his bunch,' Harpley said.

'I don't have a plan.' McCabe smiled wryly. 'I'll let things happen and just kinda go along with them. The badmen will come at me soon as they know I'm around.'

'That's not a good way of doing it.' Harpley shook his head. 'You should pick your own ground and time for a showdown.'

'I would if I knew the badmen. But I have to go out and look for them.' McCabe paused. 'If there's anything you can tell me about Gotch's bunch then I'd be happy to change my tactics. I figure Gotch has got some contacts here in town, and it would help if someone could point a finger at them.'

'I can't help you there.' Harpley shook his head. 'But there are a few men around who could be in cahoots with Gotch. I'll point them out to you shortly.'

The street door was opened and Sheriff Sarran appeared in the doorway. Lamplight glinted on the lawman's badge. Sarran's rugged face was set in harsh lines, and he nodded when he saw McCabe in the office.

'I figured they was after you soon as

I heard the shots,' he said, entering the office and closing the door. 'You did right by staying off the street.'

'I'm about to get acquainted with the town,' McCabe said.

'I'll accompany you.' Sarran eased the gun on his right thigh. 'I'll point out some of the men I suspect of likely having dealings with Gotch.'

McCabe nodded. 'I've got someone to see in about thirty minutes. Until then I'm ready to look over the town.'

Sarran opened the door of the office and stepped out on to the sidewalk. McCabe followed closely, his muscles tensed for more shooting, his hand on the butt of his holstered gun, ready to bring the weapon into play at the first sign of trouble. But the street remained silent and he closed the door of the office with a faint sigh of relief, cutting off the light shafting out of the big room.

'What can you tell me about Dave Thorn?' McCabe asked as they went along the sidewalk.

'How'd you learn about Thorn?' Sarran countered. 'You ain't been in town long enough to get information on anyone.' The sheriff paused but McCabe remained silent, and Sarran shrugged. 'Thorn is a gambler,' he resumed. 'He works Grant's saloon on a percentage. I'd give him his marching orders if I could find something to pin on him but he keeps his nose clean.'

'Was there something wrong about his takeover of the Dean spread?'

'Ah! Billy's been talking to you. That young hothead is storing up trouble for himself. I'm doing my best to keep him out of hot water, but he's intent on tangling with Thorn, and he'll surely get himself killed.'

'Never mind Billy. What about the takeover?'

'If it was fixed then Thorn did a good job of it. Art Pell, the lawyer, handled the paperwork, and I went over it with him and couldn't find anything wrong. Ash Tolliver, the banker, showed me Dean's account.

The purchase price was deposited there all right, and I saw where it had been deducted from Thorn's account. It was all above board, as it should be with men like Pell and Tolliver handling the deal. Nothing can convince me that the lawyer and the banker are crooked. Young Billy has got a bee in his bonnet about his pa's death and he don't listen to reason.'

'But it could have been rigged.' McCabe glanced around into the dense shadows, his right hand resting lightly on the butt of his gun. His hard gaze probed the darkness and his ears were strained for hostile sound.

'Sure it could! But there's no evidence, and that's what I have to work on.'

They reached the batwings of a saloon and paused to peer inside. The long room was brightly lit. There was a bar on the right-hand side, and the rest of the space was occupied by small tables.

'That tall guy behind the bar in the

smart suit is Jed Grant,' Sarran said. 'He owns this place and the livery barn. He seems fair and law-abiding. But he has an understanding with Thorn, who's at that table in the far left corner. It's probably a straight business deal between them, but I don't cotton to Grant because he works with Thorn, who has all the earmarks of being a wrong 'un.'

McCabe studied the corner table that Sarran had indicated. There were six men, including Thorn, seated around it, and they looked like the leading businessmen of the town. Apparently it was a high-class game, and all six were intent upon the play.

'What about undesirables?' McCabe asked. 'There must be some men around who don't work but have money, and they would frequent the saloon. I've found they're the most likely to be mixed up in local wrong-doing.'

'You're right. There's a few of that kind in every town in the West. I got a couple here, but they're cute. If they are working with outlaws then I ain't been able to catch them out. Jabez Eke does odd jobs around town. I figure he's behind some of the minor robberies that have occurred, but I can't prove it. And there's Barney Todd. He works at the livery barn, when he ain't drunk. It was reported to me a couple of months ago that Todd was found in the back of the general store in suspicious circumstances. Pete Donovan, who owns the store, wanted Todd charged with attempted robbery. But it looked to me that Todd was only looking for some place to lay his head after taking on a skinful of likker.'

'I figure Gotch would have someone above suspicion as their contact,' mused McCabe. 'Care for a drink, Sheriff?'

'A beer.' Sarran pushed through the batwings.

McCabe looked around alertly as he followed the lawman to the bar. There were at least a score of men in the big room, and the sound of their voices was loud. But the volume dropped when the sheriff was spotted, and Sarran smiled as he looked at McCabe.

'It's a sure sign there's trouble around when men stop talking at the sight of me,' he said. 'I just wish I could put my finger on the sore spot. But mebbe your arrival will turn up something. You've made a good start against Gotch, McCabe.'

'Have you sent someone out to locate that second outlaw I shot?' McCabe asked.

'My chief deputy, Al Spooner, rode out soon as he was ready. He's a good man. I'd trust him with my life.'

McCabe bought two beers, and Jed Grant, the saloonman, came along the bar. He was tall and lean, hard-looking, in his fifties and dressed in a brown store suit. His fleshy face shone in the lamplight. His sparse dark hair was short and flat to his skull, and his brown eyes were narrowed, filled with speculation as he looked at McCabe. There was an air of prosperity about

Jed Grant, and as he greeted Sarran in a tight, rasping tone, he lit a slim black cigar.

'Any luck hunting Gotch, Josh?' he asked hoarsely.

'You heard what happened today?' Sarran countered. He jerked a thumb at McCabe. 'Well here's the man who did it. Shot up the Gotch gang. He killed one of them and hit two more.'

'That sure was lucky.' Grant indicated their beer. 'Drink up and have one on the house. We don't get news like that every day.'

'It wasn't luck,' McCabe said firmly. 'It was down to information, which is why Gotch does so well around here. He's got someone in town telling him what's going on.'

'You got any idea who could be back of that?' Grant frowned and shook his head. His eyes were impassive. 'I don't figure it's anyone I know.'

'It could be someone we all know,' Sarran observed, and Grant nodded slowly.

McCabe drank his beer, and glanced at the big clock ticking loudly on the wall behind the bar. He set down his glass and squared his shoulders.

'I've got things to do,' he said to Sarran. 'See you later, Sheriff.'

Sarran nodded and McCabe went to the batwings and departed swiftly. Out on the sidewalk he stepped to one side of the doorway and placed his back against the front wall of the saloon. Dense shadows were crowding him, and he narrowed his gaze to take in his surroundings. The town was quiet — too quiet, he mused. But all that would soon change. He set off back to the Wells Fargo office, where he was due to meet Rosie Dean.

He heard the sound of footsteps rapping the board-walk at his back and stepped sideways into an alley on his right. He turned swiftly and leaned forward to get a glimpse of whoever was behind him. A woman's figure loomed up out of the darkness, and for a brief moment she was silhouetted against one of the lamps in front of the saloon. He thought he recognized Rosie Dean, and was about to step out of the alley to confront the girl when a figure showed up behind her. He heard her gasp of shock as someone caught hold of her arm.

'Slow down, Rosie,' a man said hoarsely. 'What's the all-fired hurry? I got word for you. Dave wants to see you in about an hour. He'll be in his hotel room. He says not to let anyone see you going in.'

'You can tell Thorn I don't take his orders,' the girl snapped, jerking herself free of the man's restraining grasp. 'He can go jump in the creek. You'd better leave me alone, Conn. There's a real man turned up in town, and by the look of him he's gonna make everyone around here dance to his tune.'

'You mean the Wells Fargo detective? Haw Haw! He ain't got a chance. He'll likely be dead come morning.' The man laughed harshly and turned away, and McCabe caught a glimpse of his silhouette against the saloon lamp as he moved. He was tall and heavily built.

The girl continued along the sidewalk towards the Wells Fargo office and McCabe remained in concealment until she had passed him. Then he moved out of the alley and followed the man who had accosted her. The big figure shouldered its way through the batwings of the saloon, and McCabe hurried forward to peer in over the double door. The man was walking to the rear of the saloon, and took up a position behind Dave Thorn's chair.

McCabe entered the saloon and went to the sheriff's side. Grant moved away behind the bar as McCabe approached, and the sheriff finished his drink and wiped his mouth as he turned to leave.

'You're soon back.' Sarran paused and leaned an elbow on the bar, gazing intently at McCabe.

'Yeah. I got things to do, but I wanta know who's the guy standing behind Thorn's chair over there. The big man wearing the red shirt.'

The sheriff glanced over his shoulder. 'That's Blade Conn, Grant's trouble shooter. Watch out if you ever tangle with him. He carries a knife in a sheath down the back of his neck, and he can pull it and stick it in a man faster than most men can draw a gun. He's another reason why I don't like or trust Grant.'

'Thanks for the tip.' McCabe studied Conn for a moment before turning away. 'See you later,' he said in parting.

Once more on the sidewalk, McCabe went along to the Wells Fargo office, covered by the dense shadows. His thoughts were busy as he tried to make something of the impressions he had gained since reaching town, aware that he could not permit himself to be side-tracked by minor issues unrelated to his job. He was here to destroy the Gotch gang. Yet he knew that any crookedness in town could be connected with the gang of coach robbers, and he went on, eager to get to grips with the lawless element.

When he entered the Wells Fargo office he paused in surprise for Rosie Dean was not there, and neither was her brother. Willard Harpley was seated behind the desk, smoking a pipe and evidently deep in thought. The Wells Fargo area manager looked up at McCabe, and then stirred and put down his pipe.

'Where's Rosie and Billy?' McCabe demanded, wondering if Harpley himself was as honest as he appeared to be.

'Rosie showed up a few moments ago and she was in a tearing hurry.' Harpley shrugged his wide shoulders. 'She took Billy by the shoulder and they went off almost at a run. What's going on? That gal was one spooked filly, McCabe.'

'I saw her on the sidewalk a few minutes ago and she was on her way to see me here.' McCabe frowned. What had happened in those few minutes to change the girl's attitude? Had she met someone else who talked her out of it? He shook his head. 'Where does she live? I have to see her before I do anything else. What she has to tell might help me in my job.'

'She's got a cabin on the edge of town, down by the creek. Do you want me to show you the way?'

'Sure. I need to get a lead on the minor badmen around here. I figure Gotch must have some of them on his payroll, and if I latch on to them I could find an easy trail to Gotch himself.'

'That's good thinking.' Harpley got to his feet. 'I'd like to hear what Rosie has to say. She sure came up against some crookedness when her pa was killed, and it was a mighty strange business. I don't think the sheriff did as much as he could have in that case. But then he needs proof before he can act, and there was no evidence against anyone.'

They left the office and Harpley led

the way along the street. Darkness was dense over the town, and there were few street lamps illuminating the area. Some buildings had lanterns burning outside and they provided dim light to show McCabe where they were walking. But he experienced a pang of uneasiness as they moved out of town.

'What doesn't make sense about the Dean business is that Frank Dean was against selling up and moving out,' Harpley remarked. 'I heard him say so myself, more than once. Then he was killed, shot in the back out on the range, and it was said that he had sold out to Dave Thorn. He was supposed to be staying on running the place for Thorn, and the selling price was in his bank account. His killer was never caught although the sheriff carried out a big search. Sarran was asking questions around the county for weeks but never learned anything. Dean's death was a complete mystery. No one ever came forward with any evidence and nothing was turned up.'

'But someone knows what happened,' McCabe mused, 'and I'd sure like to get to the bottom of it.'

'Young Billy is still het up about the murder, and he's sure Dave Thorn had something to do with it. I gave Billy a job partly to keep him out of trouble, but at times he rages about Thorn, and I wouldn't be surprised if one day he snaps and does something stupid.'

'Like trying to kill Thorn?' McCabe shook his head as he glanced around, recalling his own youthful rage and despair when his parents were murdered. He felt a pang of sympathy for Billy Dean, and firmed his resolve to do what he could to help, so long as his actions were compatible with his duty to Wells Fargo.

They reached the edge of town and Harpley paused. 'There's no light in the Dean cabin,' he said.

'I can't even see a cabin,' McCabe responded, narrowing his eyes.

'There are half a dozen shacks scattered along the bank of the creek.

The Dean cabin is the only one that can be seen from here, and if there was a light in it you'd be able to spot it. I don't think Rosie and Billy came here.'

'Let's check. Perhaps they've got the window covered.'

They closed in on the cabin, which loomed up out of the darkness, and when McCabe finally saw the indistinct outline of the small building his keen gaze also caught a flicker of movement at the left front corner. It was just a slight alteration in the pattern of dense shadows but instantly his sense of preservation assumed control. He uttered a warning to Harpley and threw himself sideways to the ground, his right hand flashing to the butt of his holstered gun, and the weapon was in his grasp when he hit the ground, his right thumb pulling back the hammer.

Two orange gun-flashes split the shadows by the corner of the cabin, one low to the ground as if the ambusher were kneeling, and the other about waist high on a standing man. The crackle of closely passing slugs sounded in McCabe's right ear. He thumbed off a reply instantly, blinking against the gun flash, but even so his sight was dazzled, and he rolled to his left and came up into the aim again, blinking rapidly as he bracketed the corner of the cabin with three probing shots. Then he got to one knee, gun muzzle lifted in readiness while listening to the fading echoes of the shooting.

There was movement at the corner of the cabin and he saw an indistinct figure detach itself from the surrounding shadows and come forward an unsteady step. McCabe lifted his gun to cover the man, but held his fire, and a sigh escaped him as the figure collapsed to the ground and lay still.

He heard the sound of running feet receding quickly into the background beyond the cabin and got up slowly, gun cocked, his finger trembling against the trigger. Then he heard the rapid tattoo of departing hooves. He nodded.

That figured. He went forward cautiously, covering the motionless figure on the ground, satisfied with what he had. If he could identify just one of these ambushers he would be in business.

'What was that all about?' Harpley asked, coming to McCabe's side. 'There were two of them, and they must have been waiting for you, except that no one knew you were coming here.'

'Yeah.' McCabe dropped to one knee beside the motionless figure, his gun covering it. He used his left hand to touch the man's chest and his fingers encountered a sticky patch of blood on a rough shirt. There was no sign of a heartbeat, and his lips pulled tight as he sat back on his heels. 'He's dead,' he informed Harpley. 'You got a match? I wanta see his face.'

'It's too dangerous to show a light,' Harpley warned.

'I'll cover you.' McCabe got to his feet and moved forward until the body was behind him. He faced the darkness and dropped into a crouch, the muzzle of his gun weaving slightly as he covered the area.

Harpley struck a match and held it close to the face of the dead man. McCabe concentrated on what he was doing, and heard Harpley utter a gasp of surprise.

'What is it?' he demanded. 'Is he someone you know?'

Harpley extinguished the match and stood up. He bumped against McCabe in the darkness, and McCabe eased back a pace.

'I know him all right.' Harpley spoke in a rasping tone. 'It's Al Spooner.'

McCabe frowned. 'I've heard that name mentioned since I came to town,' he mused. 'Who is he?'

'The sheriff's chief deputy.'

'The hell you say!' McCabe fought down his rising shock. 'Sarran sent him out to check on the outlaw I downed from the coach. What is he doing skulking around town?'

'And shooting at folks without

warning,' Harpley added.

McCabe exhaled slowly as he reloaded the spent chambers in his gun and then holstered the weapon. Some of the events that were occuring did not add up, and he was puzzled by the apparent contradictions in evidence. Why had Rosie Dean suddenly taken flight? Had she lost her nerve? She had sounded confident when accosted by Grant's trouble shooter, Blade Conn, but moments later she had hurried into the Wells Fargo office, collected her young brother and hightailed it into the night. And the chief deputy sheriff had been waiting outside the girl's cabin, opening fire without warning and apparently with the intention of killing. Who had he been expecting? Rosie Dean or McCabe himself?

'You've stirred up a real mess of stew,' Harpley observed. 'We'd better toss this problem into Sarran's lap and see what he can make of it.'

'I'm wondering about the second drygulcher,' McCabe mused. 'He sure high-tailed it in a hurry, and as far as I know, Spooner rode out of town alone. Did he intend to carry out the sheriff's orders or was he intent on another chore first, like killing me?' McCabe shook his head. 'There are easier ways of doing that than waiting out here, hoping I'd show up. No one knew I'd come here. Hell, I didn't even know myself until a few minutes ago.'

'The first thing you've gotta do is find Rosie Dean,' Harpley suggested. 'Perhaps she knows something.'

McCabe nodded and holstered in his gun, grimacing at the tang of gunsmoke in his nostrils. Looking towards the lights of town, he tensed when he saw a lantern being carried towards them amidst several swiftly moving but indistinct figures. The next moment a harsh voice called out.

'You by the cabin. Stand still. Who fired those shots?'

'That sounds like Sarran,' Harpley commented, and, raising his voice, shouted his name.

McCabe remained silent, his thoughts busy trying to unravel the undercurrents of the unfolding events. But he did not have sufficient background knowledge to grasp facts, and controlled his impatience. That knowledge would come when he began to operate, but it was already obvious that a more complex situation existed here than the capture of a few coach robbers.

4

The sheriff cursed long and loudly when he saw his dead deputy, and there was consternation in the voices of the two men accompanying the lawman.

'What was he doing around here when I sent him out to check on that outlaw you downed on the trail?' Sarran demanded.

'Why did he start shooting at us without warning?' Harpley rapped. 'And there was another man was with him but he got away.'

'Give me the lantern.' McCabe held out his hand. 'I wanta look for tracks. That other galoot sure rode out fast.' He took the lantern from the sheriff and moved to the corner of the cabin, where he dropped to his haunches and held the lantern a few inches above the dust. 'Look,' he observed. 'Spots of blood. I hit the second guy as well.'

There was more and more blood on the trampled ground, and McCabe went quickly along the side of the cabin. He pulled up short when he saw a horse standing with trailing reins behind the cabin, and the sheriff spoke quickly.

'That's Spooner's buckskin. What in tarnation was he doing around here when he should have been out on the trail?'

McCabe was more interested in the tracks of the horse that had left the scene so quickly, and crouched again, holding the lantern close to the ground and shielding his eyes against the glare as he looked for sign.

'There's more blood here,' he announced. 'I reckon this guy needs a doctor real bad.' He checked the deep hoof-prints heading away from the rear of the cabin, examining them closely. 'The left hind shoe has a piece missing on the outer edge,' he mused. 'It should be easy to track or find.' He straightened and handed the lantern back to the shocked lawman. 'I wanta check the livery barn in case this galoot rode in there.'

'I'll go with you,' Harpley said instantly. 'I want to get to the bottom of this.'

'So Spooner shot at you without warning,' Sarran mused. His face was pale in the yellow lamplight, his eyes slitted, filled with reflected brightness.

Harpley gave his view of the short exchange of fire, and it tallied with what McCabe had seen.

'If it wasn't for McCabe's gun speed we'd have both been hit,' the Wells Fargo manager said harshly. 'Spooner was intent on killing. But whether he knew who he was shooting at is something you'll have to discover, Josh, and I don't envy you the task. This business is getting more puzzling by the minute.'

They left the sheriff considering his dead deputy's last actions and Harpley led the way along the street. There were a number of men moving towards the scene of the shooting, and McCabe felt a tingling of impatience in the back of his mind. He wanted to get to grips with the Gotch gang, but what was happening around town seemed to be side-tracking him. But he could not be sure of that yet, and had to play the grim game by ear until he gained enough hard facts to decide.

When they reached the stable the liveryman was standing just inside the big, gloomy barn. He was a tall, thin, beanpole of a man, dressed in dusty trousers and a ragged jacket. A stained black hat was pulled low over his forehead. and brown, gimlet eyes gazed from under the wide brim. He stared at McCabe with unusual interest, and kept looking at him even when Harpley spoke.

'You had anyone ride in here within the last ten minutes, Mort,' the Wells Fargo manager demanded.

'Just a couple of cowpunchers, in from the JS ranch.'

'Was one of them bleeding, mebbe?' McCabe asked.

'Bleeding? Say, I heard shots some time back. So what happened? You're the Wells Fargo detective everyone is talking about, ain't yuh?'

'What about newcomers, Mort?' Harpley cut in.

'I told you. A couple of Joel Slater's riders showed up. If you had trouble with someone and he's bleeding then he ain't likely to ride in here. You should check out Doc Miller's place. Anyone with a bullet in him is likely to head there, huh?'

'How many horses you got in the barn?' McCabe demanded.

'Nigh on twenty.' The liveryman pushed back his battered Stetson. 'You looking for any particular animal?'

'Bring a lantern and we'll give them the once-over.' McCabe spoke impatiently, sensing that the liveryman was uneasy about something, and he flexed the fingers of his right hand, his instincts warning him to be careful.

The man obeyed, and Harpley watched while McCabe made a round of every horse in the barn, checking the left hind foot of each animal. Twice McCabe paused and asked for the name of the owner of a particular animal, and the liveryman answered seemingly reluctantly. Harpley remained silent, and when McCabe had finished checking the horses the Wells Fargo manager raised an eyebrow in a silent question. McCabe nodded slowly and walked back along the row of tethered horses until he reached a sorrel. He patted the animal's flank.

'Who did you say owns this horse?' he demanded.

The liveryman stared at him, his expression suddenly grim, and he shifted his weight from one foot to the other.

'I don't rightly know,' he said uneasily. 'It came in earlier in the day, while I was busy elsewhere. Can't say I've seen it around before.'

'How long have you been in the

barn?' McCabe asked.

'Mebbe a couple of hours. What are you getting at?'

'This horse left tracks in the dust near a cabin we were visiting a few minutes ago, and the rider was dripping blood when he rode out.' McCabe peered at the ground around the horse and his keen gaze soon picked out droplets of fresh blood on the straw that had been put down as bedding for the animal. 'Why are you lying, mister? And you look scared to hell about something.'

'I ain't lying.' Bluster crept into the liveryman's harsh voice. 'You can't accuse me of helping an outlaw.'

'Who said he's an outlaw, Mort?' demanded Harpley.

'He can't be up to any good if you shot him. You're both Wells Fargo men, and everyone knows the company has been getting trouble from outlaws. Don't try to drag me into this. I only take care of the horses that are brung in.'

'Did you see the man who rode in?' McCabe persisted.

'Lemme see.' The liveryman made a big show of trying to remember, then shook his head. 'Can't say I did. I been a mite busy here. Perhaps Pete tended him. You'll have to ask Pete. He went off duty an hour ago.'

A piece of straw suddenly floated down from the loft over their heads and McCabe was aware of a scuffling sound above him. He looked up, saw a cloud of dust coming down from the loft, and his holstered gun seemed to leap out of leather and into his right hand. He moved back a couple of paces, angling the muzzle of his gun at the loft. Harpley moved quickly, drawing his sixgun and crouching. The liveryman cowered behind the horse.

'Who's up there in the loft?' McCabe demanded, his voice crackling through the heavy silence.

A sixgun thundered deafeningly over their heads and the barn was filled with blasting echoes. A bullet splintered a post beside McCabe, and he ducked and turned to run across the barn, twisting to look up into the open-sided loft. Blue gunsmoke was drifting slowly, and he turned his gun on the spot and bracketed it with three swift shots.

A man staggered forward into view, a gun spilling from his hand, and he pitched forward over the edge of the floor of the loft and thudded heavily on the hard-packed floor beside Harpley, who sprang back in alarm. McCabe was covering the figure, and saw that the man was dead. Blood was staining his shirt front in two places in the centre of his chest, and there was a big stain of blood at his right shoulder.

'I couldn't tell you about him,' the ostler said agitatedly, his thin tone cutting through the fading echoes of the shooting. 'He came in some minutes ago, and I could see he was a hardcase. He was bleeding bad from that shoulder wound. He told me to stay in one place where he could cover me, and went up into the loft. Before I could think of what to do you came along.'

'Any idea who he is?' McCabe demanded.

'I ain't seen him before.' Harpley shook his head.

'I seen him around,' the liveryman said. 'He's usually with two or three other hardcases.'

'Any of his pards in town now?' McCabe persisted.

'Yeah. One is. The two of them rode in earlier. They was in town a couple of hours before this one came back for his horse.'

'About the time Al Spooner rode out?' Harpley asked, and McCabe nodded to himself.

'That's right.' The liveryman looked puzzled. 'How'd you know that?'

'Have you seen anything of Rosie Dean and her brother Billy?' McCabe asked.

'Hell no! They wouldn't come in here. They don't own horses.'

There was a noise just outside the big

front door of the barn and then Sheriff Sarran appeared in the doorway, gun in hand. He paused on the threshold, eyes slitted against the yellow glare of the lanterns, then came to where McCabe was standing.

'Heard the shots,' he commented. 'Who's this?' He toed the dead man.

'You don't know him, Josh?' Harpley countered.

'Seen him around town a few times. He's one of those men you were asking about, McCabe. Always got money in his pocket but doesn't have a regular job.'

'One of his pards is in town now,' McCabe said. 'The liveryman knows him by sight, and he was about to go with us to point him out.' He looked at the stableman. 'Isn't that right?'

'Sure thing! Anything to help.' The man nodded although reluctance had sounded in his voice.

Townsmen were beginning to gather outside the barn, crowding the doorway and asking questions. Sarran shook his head. His face was suddenly looking drawn and old, and he heaved a long sigh as he took charge.

'I figure to handle this now,' he said, looking into McCabe's eyes. 'But all I've seemed to be doing since you arrived is follow in your footsteps.'

'I have got other things to do.' McCabe spoke easily. 'I wanta know what happened to Rosie Dean and her brother Billy. I don't figure they should have disappeared like they did.'

'I'll chase that up too,' Sarran insisted. He shook his head slowly, his lips a thin line in his leathery face. 'Come on, Mort, let's see if we can find the pard of this dead hardcase.'

McCabe walked out of the barn and the townsmen parted to let him through their dense ranks. Harpley silently accompanied him, and it was not until they were walking along the sidewalk into the centre of town that the Wells Fargo manager spoke.

'What you got in mind to do now, Cole?' he asked.

'Like I said, Rosie and Billy must be located. But I've got to get some sleep so I'm fit to ride out tomorrow to pick up Gotch's trail. That's the reason I'm here. Gotch's bunch.'

Harpley nodded. 'I guess you've got the bull by the horns. As to Rosie and Billy. Where in hell could they have got to? That girl was steamed up about something when she came into the office ahead of you. It don't make sense, her vanishing like that.'

'As far as we know she hasn't vanished,' McCabe mused. 'But something mighty important must have happened to keep her out of sight.'

'You figure someone might have grabbed her and Billy?'

'I don't know. But she was supposed to see Dave Thorn in his hotel room later. I thought she and Billy looked on Thorn as their father's killer.'

'Billy was always saying something like that, but I never heard Rosie breathe a word about her father. She sure didn't like Thorn though. But I think she had enough sense to keep her mouth shut. She knew something bad could happen to her if she spoke out of turn. That's the way of it around here these days. But I got a feeling all that is about to change.'

'Where is Thorn's room? At the hotel?'

'Yeah. You wanta check it out?' Harpley sounded eager. 'I'll go along with you.'

'Rosie's problem doesn't look like it's connected with our business,' McCabe mused. 'But someone around here is helping Gotch with information, and that someone could be handling a little extra crookedness on the side.'

'I agree with you.' Harpley nodded. 'In any case, Billy works for Wells Fargo and we have a reputation for looking after our employees. If Billy is in trouble then I wanta know about it.'

They continued along the street until they reached the big hotel, and Harpley paused and pointed up to a lighted window on the right-hand corner of the building.

'That's Thorn's room,' he said, 'and there's a light in it. So mebbe we'd better call on Thorn and see who's with him.'

'Which is exactly what I plan to do.' McCabe dropped his hand to his gun and eased the weapon in its holster.

They went into the hotel and Harpley spoke to the small man behind the reception desk.

'Hi, Ed. Is Dave Thorn in?'

'Yeah. Came in about five minutes ago.' The hotel clerk was dressed in a neat store suit. He was well under six feet in height, neat-looking, small-boned and thin. His lean face was pock-marked, his dark eyes sunk well back in their sockets. He had a look about him of not getting out into the open air enough, McCabe mused.

'Was he alone?' Harpley persisted.

'Yep. He's on his own.'

'Has Rosie Dean come in here recently?' McCabe asked.

The clerk shook his head slowly. 'I ain't seen her,' he said hesitantly.

'You don't seem too sure about that,' McCabe observed.

'I'm sure all right. Just surprised by the question, that's all. We don't have women wandering in and out of this hotel, day or night.'

'We got some business with Thorn,' said Harpley.

'He didn't say he was expecting anyone.' The clerk stiffened his shoulders as if about to deny them access, then met McCabe's cold gaze and exhaled slowly and shook his head. 'But go right on up,' he invited.

Harpley led the way up the stairs, and the sound of their boots echoed hollowly on the floorboards. They walked along a corridor, and McCabe, looking ahead and ready for trouble, saw a man emerge from a room almost at the end of the corridor. The newcomer came swiftly towards them, and McCabe experienced a shock when he looked at the man's weatherbeaten face and recognized Rattlesnake Riley, one of the prominent members of the Gotch gang.

McCabe put his left hand on Harpley's shoulder and jerked him to a halt in midstride. Harpley uttered an ejaculation and quickly glanced at McCabe, then froze into immobility when he saw McCabe's intent manner. He followed McCabe's gaze and looked at Riley, now only a few yards away, and the outlaw was gazing suspiciously at them.

Riley had the instincts of a wild animal, and possibly sensed a trap. He paused, dropping a hand uncertainly to the flared butt of the sixgun on his right hip. McCabe instantly palmed his gun, and the three clicks as he cocked the weapon sounded inordinately loud in the close atmosphere. Riley instinctively began to lift his own gun, but when McCabe's muzzle gaped at his chest from a range of three yards he thrust his weapon back into its holster and lifted his hands shoulder high, his face filled with enquiry.

'What's this, a hold-up?' he demanded in a rasping tone.

'You're under arrest, Riley,' McCabe told him. 'Keep your hands high.'

Harpley went to one side and jerked Riley's gun from its holster. McCabe moved in a pace, his gun steady. He waited while Harpley searched the outlaw, and smiled when a long-bladed knife was taken out of a sheath on the back of Riley's gun-belt.

'You're making a big mistake,' Riley said harshly. 'You've got the wrong man. My name ain't Riley. I'm Wade Collins, from Montana. I'm a cattle buyer, and I was visiting Dave Thorn, who owns a cow spread in this neck of the woods. You don't have to take my word for it. Thorn is in that room along there. Ask him who I am. He can tell you.'

'I know who you are, and we're calling on Thorn,' McCabe said. 'Get down on your belly, Riley, and stretch out your arms full length, palms flat to the floor. Don't twitch a muscle or you'll collect a slug. Watch him, Harpley, and shoot him if he tries anything.'

Harpley moved back a couple of paces as Riley got down on the floor. McCabe stepped over the outlaw and went on to the door of the room from which he had seen Riley appear. Gun in his right hand, McCabe softly tried the door handle, and drew a swift breath when the door opened. He stepped into the room and paused on the threshold, his gun covering the interior.

Dave Thorn was seated on the single bed in the room, which was over by the window, and the gambler looked up swiftly at McCabe's entrance. His right hand moved quickly towards his left shoulder, but stopped when McCabe thumbed back his hammer.

'What's the meaning of this?' Thorn demanded.

'You'll find out shortly. On your feet, and keep your hands wide of your body. We're going along to the law office, where we can talk and what you say can be noted. Just stand still while I draw your fangs.'

McCabe went forward and checked Thorn carefully, removing a small hideout gun from a shoulder holster in the gambler's left armpit. Then he stepped backwards a pace and studied Thorn's taut features.

'Why did you wanta see Rosie Dean here at this time?' McCabe asked.

'What's that to you?' Thorn countered harshly. 'You might be a Wells Fargo detective, but that don't give you the right to stick your nose into my personal business.'

'Rattlesnake Riley, a known outlaw, came out of this room a few moments ago. What was your business with him?'

'Who in hell is Rattlesnake Riley?' Thorn shook his head. 'A man named Wade Collins, cattle buyer from Montana, left me a few moments ago. We were talking cattle business.

You better get outa here before I make a complaint to the local law. You ain't got the right to come busting in here asking questions.'

'You know where the jail is,' McCabe said. 'Make for it, and don't try anything or you'll wind up dead. He stepped aside as Thorn came towards the door, and followed the gambler out to the corridor.

Thorn paused when he saw Riley stretched out on the floor with Willard Harpley menacing him with a drawn gun. He threw a glance over his shoulder at McCabe, who motioned with his gun for the gambler to keep moving. Harpley told Riley to get up, and the outlaw joined the gambler and they descended the stairs to the hotel lobby.

McCabe felt as though he was walking on thin ice. He did not like taking prisoners in this way. But he was ready for any trickery, and his trigger finger was trembling with eagerness as he and Harpley ushered the two men

99

out of the hotel and along the sidewalk towards the jail.

'Just don't make the mistake of thinking you can get away,' he warned when Thorn paused in the shadows and half turned to him.

'You're making a big mistake, and the laugh will be on you when the truth comes out,' Thorn blustered.

'And you'd like to spare my feelings, huh?' McCabe laughed. 'Save it for the sheriff. He's the man you'll have to convince.'

They reached the jail and Harpley went forward to open the door. McCabe kept his gun on the prisoners, who filed into the office under the threat of the ready weapon. Sarran was seated at his desk, and looked up enquiringly at the newcomers.

'We didn't have no luck looking for that man Mort mentioned,' the sheriff said. 'He must have left town in a hurry.' He fell silent as he took in details of Riley's appearance. 'Say, ain't that one of Sam Gotch's bunch?'

'Rattlesnake Riley himself,' said Harpley. 'McCabe spotted him right off and got the drop on him.'

'He was visiting Thorn at the hotel.' McCabe explained the circumstances.

Sarran picked up a bunch of keys off the desk and led the way into the cell block. 'Let's put them where they'll be safe and then we can talk about it,' he said. 'I'm sure glad to see Riley, but I ain't so sure about Thorn. What for you picked him up? I figger he's crooked through to the backbone, but my experience is that he's too slippery to let anything be pinned on him.'

'I didn't know this man is an outlaw, if that is what he is,' Thorn said sharply. 'I thought he was a cattle buyer from Montana. He told me his name is Wade Collins. There's gonna be trouble over this, Sheriff.'

'We can check out your story,' Sarran said. 'But right now you'll have to stay in jail, so don't give me no trouble.'

The prisoners were locked in separate cells, and McCabe heaved a long sigh as he holstered his gun. He led the way back into the office and leaned his shoulder against the street door.

'Looks like we've got the man who's been supplying the outlaws with information,' he said. 'We got Thorn dead to rights.'

'I'll check him out for sure,' Sarran replied. 'But what about the rest of Gotch's bunch? Do you figure they're around town as well?'

'It wouldn't hurt to make a search,' Harpley said eagerly. 'But there are a lot of details we don't have, and at the moment we can't take anything at face value.'

'I'm concerned about Rosie and Billy Dean.' McCabe's face was grim. 'It looks like they disappeared. I heard Blade Conn tell Rosie to be at Thorn's room about this time, and she was supposed to meet me at the Wells Fargo office earlier.' He glanced enquiringly at Harpley, who nodded.

'She sure came into the office but was in a tearing hurry,' Harpley corroborated. 'She took Billy and went off fast.'

'We'll find her.' Sarran nodded. 'Then perhaps we can begin to make some sense out of this business.'

McCabe straightened wearily. 'It's in your hands now, Sheriff,' he said. stifling a yawn. 'I'm gonna hit the sack. I wanta be out on the trail come daylight, and when I pick up Gotch's tracks there's no telling where they'll lead me. The coach driver said he was gonna book me a room at the hotel. You'll be able to find me there until sun-up, if you've got anything to tell me. After that, anything happening around town will have to wait until I return.'

He departed then, his mind buzzing with the developments that had occurred. Harpley left him at the hotel and McCabe saw the little clerk and got the key to his room. He was deadly tired, and, once secure in the room, took off his boots and dropped upon the bed to lie unmoving until the sun peeped in at the window just after dawn the next morning.

5

McCabe's thoughts were sober as he prepared to face the day. He washed and shaved, then cleaned his sixgun. When he was ready to start working he left the room and went down to the lobby. A middle-aged woman wearing a long black dress was standing behind the desk, and she gazed critically at him for a moment.

'Good morning,' she greeted. 'Would you like breakfast now?'

'I shall need a good meal before I set about my chores,' he replied.

'The dining-room is across the lobby. If you go in and sit down my husband will take your order.'

McCabe entered the small dining-room and sat down at the nearest table. The clerk who had been at the desk the previous evening came into the room through an inner doorway, and he remained silent while taking McCabe's order.

'Nice place you've got here,' McCabe ventured.

'It does good business,' came the non-committal reply. 'I hope you slept well last night.'

'I shall recommend the hotel to all my friends,' McCabe said wryly.

The clerk departed quickly, and McCabe looked over his shoulder when he heard voices out in the lobby. Sheriff Sarran came into the dining-room, and nodded when he saw McCabe. He came across and sat down opposite him.

'I was hoping to see you before you left town,' he said. His face was set in harsh lines and he looked as if he had not slept at all during the night. 'I got some news that won't sit too well with you.'

McCabe regarded the sheriff with expressionless face, but his thoughts were harsh.

'Well hit me with it,' he said tersely.

'I've got a strong stomach.'

'I found Billy Dean about an hour ago.' Sarran shook his head slowly, his lips drawn tightly against his teeth. His eyes were bloodshot and weariness occupied every line and seam of his weathered face. 'The boy is dead — knife-wound between his shoulder-blades. Doc Miller reckons he was killed around midnight.'

A coldness settled in the pit of McCabe's stomach as he visualized Billy's youthful face and heard the boy's eager voice in his mind. He clenched his teeth against unaccustomed emotion, and drew a deep breath as he gazed at the sheriff.

'Have you got anything on who did it?' he asked.

'Nary a thing.' Sarran shook his head. 'Almost anyone could have knifed him. He wasn't seen around town after Rosie took him out of the Wells Fargo office.'

'That would be about two hours before he died,' McCabe observed.

'You've got to find out what he did and where he went during those two hours, Sheriff.'

'That's easier said than done. I been making enquiries, but no one is talking.' Sarran's voice tremored. He was apparently badly shaken by Billy's death.

McCabe's breakfast was brought in by a young woman, and she seemed distressed as she placed the loaded plate in front of him.

'Morning, Sheriff,' she said softly. 'I just heard about Billy Dean. Who could have done such a terrible thing?'

'Molly, I'm gonna find out if it's the last thing I do,' Sarren replied.

'He was such a nice, helpful boy. You should check up on Dave Thorn. He was always saying that something bad would happen to Billy if he didn't stop making allegations.' The girl departed, and Sarran shook his head.

'You figure Thorn could be involved in this?' McCabe asked. 'He sent a message to Rosie Dean to see him in his room at ten last evening.'

'But she didn't turn up there. You were at the hotel about that time.'

'And we picked up Rattlesnake Riley. If Thorn wanted Billy dead, who do you figure he would use to do the chore?'

Sarran gazed at McCabe for several moments, shaking his head slowly, his eyes inscrutable. Then he sighed again. 'It won't help to speculate,' he said. 'But Blade Conn is Thorn's dirty-job man.'

'And Conn is fond of using a knife, huh?' McCabe began to eat mechanically, his mind flitting over the situation, and he was not aware of the food he was putting into his mouth. He needed to fill his belly, for when he hit the trail there was no telling when he would get the chance to eat again. Two years of working for Wells Fargo had taught him that golden rule.

'I figure it might help if I ran a bluff on Thorn,' Sarran said musingly. 'If you've got time when you've finished your breakfast perhaps you'll come along and watch.'

'Sure. Billy was a Wells Fargo employee, and the company has a big reputation for taking care of its men. Does Harpley know what's happened?'

'I called on him before coming to see you.' Sarran nodded. 'You can bet the dust will fly around town now.' He raised his voice and called for a coffee, and the waitress brought it for him.

McCabe finished his meal and got to his feet. He drew his gun and checked the weapon, nodding slowly when he caught Sarran's eye. The sheriff was grim-faced as he led the way out of the hotel.

At the jail, Sarran picked up the cell keys and led the way into the cell block. McCabe remained in the background when the sheriff paused at the door of the cell housing Dave Thorn. The gambler was seated on the foot of his single bed, head in his hands.

'You better be thinking deeply,

110

Thorn, because you've got a lot to answer for.' Sarran said. 'I found Billy Dean dead on the back lot behind Grant's saloon. He'd been knifed in the back. I got word that Blade Conn was out there last night, and when I got to Conn just now he tried to make a fight of it. Before he died he said he came to that window in the back wall of your cell last night and you told him to shut Billy's mouth for good.'

'That's a damn lie!' Thorn got to his feet and came to the barred door, grasping the bars and glaring at Sarran.

'A dying man don't usually tell lies,' Sarran sneered. 'Conn backed you every which-way, Thorn, as every-one around here knows. So why would he lie with his last breath? I figure he would only lie to put you in the clear. But he told it like it was. You put him up to beefing young Billy.'

'I deny that, and there ain't nobody gonna believe the word of a dead man, especially a man like Conn. Heck, Conn might have been saying that I had nothing to do with it, and mebbe you got it wrong.'

'I had a witness with me, and he'll swear to the truth. I got you dead to rights, Thorn.' Sarran smiled grimly. 'I been hoping for a long time to get the dead-wood on you, and now I've done it. You'll be for the long drop over this, and it'll be a pleasure to put the rope around your neck.'

'I wanta see Art Pell,' Thorn rapped. 'He'll soon get me out of here.'

'You ain't seeing any one until I know what you were cooking up with Rattlesnake Riley,' Sarran retorted. 'You're up to your neck in trouble, Thorn. Birds of a feather flock together, they say, and you've got a lot of explaining to do. If you got any sense you'll come clean and tell me what's been going on. I might be able to make it easier for you if you had nothing to do with Billy Dean's murder. But as it stands right now, you're as good as hanged.'

McCabe looked around the cell block

while the sheriff was talking. He did not think the lawman could trick Thorn into revealing anything. The man was too tough for that. He looked into the next cell and saw Rattlesnake Riley lying on the bunk, eyes open and coolly regarding him.

'Riley, I'm riding out to check on the shooting that hit the coach after the attempted robbery,' he said. 'I hit two more of your gang. What happened after the coach pulled away from you?'

'Sam said we gotta put you under soon as we can,' the outlaw replied, putting his hands under his head and setting himself more comfortably on the hard bunk. 'You hit us like a one-man army, McCabe. Where in hell did you come from? And how'd you know we was planning to hit that coach at that spot and that time?'

'The same way you knew which coach to hit,' McCabe said. 'Information. I was told where to be and at what time, and sure enough your gang showed up.'

'Sam ain't a bit happy about that.' Riley shook his head. 'Somethin' bad is goin' on round here.'

'That why you were in town talking to Thorn?' McCabe asked. 'You've forgotten about being Wade Collins from Montana, huh?'

'There ain't no point lying when you know who I am.' The outlaw grimaced.

'That's a fact. I got wanted posters on you and most of the gang. I'm riding out now to pick up Gotch, and anyone who is still with him.'

'You got more than your share of gall,' Riley observed.

'I got more than gall to back my play,' McCabe told him.

Sarran turned to the door leading into the office. 'Just think over what I've told you, Thorn,' he said in parting. 'I got Conn's statement to take into court, and that will be enough to put a rope around your neck. If you've got any sense at all you'll come clean and tell me what the hell is going on around here. Riley is a hardened outlaw, and he knows when he's beaten.'

Back in the office, McCabe walked across to the large-scale map pinned to the wall behind the sheriff's cluttered desk. He studied the details, pinpointing the town and looking over the area to the south.

'That's where the coach was held up yesterday,' Sarran said, coming to his side and pointing to the map. 'And that's where you fought off Gotch and his boys on your way to town afterwards in the coach.'

'Yeah. I got that much.' McCabe nodded. 'Now fill me in on the cow spreads in the county.'

'That's the spread Thorn bought off the Deans.' Sarran tapped another spot on the map, which was also south of town.

'Do you still figure he bought that place legally?'

'I got to believe that until I get evidence that points the other way, and on the face of it Thorn has got himself covered in law all ways to the middle. He's got the local lawyer and the banker backing him up.'

'Uh-huh. We'll let that lie for now.' McCabe studied the map. 'You got any ideas where Gotch and his bunch have been hiding out? Have you tried to run him to ground after his raids? Could he be lying low on some spread out there?'

'That would mean one of the ranchers being crooked.' Sarran sounded surprised. 'I ain't never thought of that. I have tried to run Gotch and his bunch to earth, and they always hide their tracks and disappear in this area.' He tapped the map to the south. 'Whether they double back or head in some other direction I ain't been able to find out yet. That's why they've been getting away with just about everything they try.'

The street door was opened and McCabe looked round to see Willard Harpley entering the office. The Wells Fargo manager looked as if he had aged ten years overnight.

'Howdy, Cole,' Harpley greeted in a harsh tone. 'What about Billy? How'd that news sit with you?'

'We'll get whoever killed him,' McCabe said through his teeth. 'But right now I'm planning to go out after Gotch and the rest of his bunch.'

'Do you wanta take a couple of men along with you?' Harpley offered. 'I got some good men who would back your play.'

'Thanks, but I like to work alone.' McCabe shook his head. 'If I run into something I can't handle on my own I'll come back for help.' He looked at the sheriff, noting the lawman's set features and haggard eyes. 'I'll sack up some supplies and then hit the trail. I don't know how long I'll be gone, but I won't come back until I've done something about Gotch. I hope you'll find Rosie Dean, but I got a nasty feeling something bad has already happened to her, and you can bet Thorn knows about it.'

'I'll be working on that angle,' Sarran assured him. 'I ain't letting Thorn out've that cell until we know what happened last night.'

McCabe sighed with relief as he left the office with Harpley following closely.

'How far do you trust the sheriff?' McCabe asked quietly.

'I reckon we can trust him all the way.' Harpley spoke slowly, as if considering his answer. Then he nodded. 'I'd swear Josh Sarran is honest, although I had doubts when the business of the Dean ranch came up about a year ago. And Sarran is a close friend of Joel Slater, who owns the JS ranch. Slater is sitting on a water-hole that belongs to Wells Fargo. We have a way station out there. I reckon, when he gets here, Frank Holbrooke will tell you to move in and clear Slater's cowhands off that water-hole. It'll be a tough chore, Cole.'

'Tougher than nailing Gotch's bunch?' McCabe countered. He smiled. 'I take my jobs as they come, and I've never found anything easy. Now, I'm going out to pick up Gotch's trail. I've wasted too much time around here as it is. You won't know what I'm doing until I get back, and that might not be inside of a week. I won't come back unless I can't pick up Gotch's trail. One way or another, Gotch is finished around here.'

'That's the kind of talk I like to hear.' Harpley looked around the street as they reached the general store. 'I took the liberty of having your horse saddled for you. It'll be outside the Wells Fargo office when you're ready to ride.'

'Thanks.' McCabe touched the brim of his hat and entered the store. The storeman was serving a couple of women who were talking about the death of Billy Dean, and McCabe took stock of the situation as he waited, his thoughts sombre. When it was his turn he gave an order for food that would see him through several days on the range, and bought a couple of boxes of .45 cartridges for his sixgun and some .45–40 shells for his rifle.

The storeman was talkative, and McCabe listened silently as the man spoke about Billy Dean.

'It's a crying shame, the way some men get away with murder around here.' Pete Donovan was tall and thin, in his early sixties, with sparse grey hair and a bushy moustache that once had been black but was now liberally streaked with grey. 'You're the Wells Fargo detective, huh? Heard tell about you. Did a good job yesterday when the coach was held up. You was shot at by Al Spooner last night, huh? Spooner was a man hard to figger. I reckoned he was sweet on Rosie Dean. But that wouldn't be a good reason for him to shoot at you. I guess you can always tell a man by his friends, and Spooner mixed with a rough bunch when he was off duty. He always said he had to mix with crooks to do his job properly, but I'll never know why Josh Sarran picked him for a deputy. I reckon Spooner knew more about the bank raid over to Broken Tree than he ever told about. If you ask me, he was mixed up in that somewhere.'

'Tell me more.' McCabe was always eager to glean background information.

'It happened about a year ago.' Donovan was warming up. He spent most of his days chewing the fat with his customers. He heard footsteps at the door and glanced past McCabe, then abruptly fell silent and turned away quickly. 'I'll, uh, get your order now,' he said uneasily.

McCabe glanced over his shoulder and saw Blade Conn coming towards him. The big man had arrogance in his movements and expression and there was an unwholesome glitter in his dark eyes. McCabe tensed for action as Conn stopped at his side, sensing that the newcomer was on the warpath.

'I just heard that you jugged Dave Thorn last night.' Conn's thick voice was filled with barely suppressed fury.

'I figure you made a bad mistake, mister.'

'Take it up with the sheriff.' McCabe shrugged. 'It's his business, not mine. But if you wanta know, Thorn was in the company of Rattlesnake Riley, one of Sam Gotch's gang. Someone's been keeping Gotch informed, and it looks like it was Thorn.'

'I work a lot with Thorn, and I tell you it ain't him. There are some others around town you should check on before Dave. I reckon you've been given the wrong information.'

'If you've got any information about outlaws then see the sheriff,' McCabe said flatly. 'It ain't my business. Riley was my business, and when he came out of Thorn's room I had to arrest Thorn as well. They both lied about Riley's identity, and Thorn will be held until he's been checked out.'

Conn half turned towards McCabe, who fell back a pace. The big man's left hand went up to his shoulder, and McCabe remembered the warning that Conn carried a knife in a sheath hanging down between his shoulder-blades. With a speed that was surprising, Conn grasped the haft of a knife and began to draw it. McCabe set his right hand into action, and when Conn felt the prod of a gun muzzle against his stomach he paused, his action with the knife only half completed. Turning his gaze downwards, Conn froze when he saw McCabe's sixgun levelled at him, and when McCabe cocked the weapon the big man raised his hands.

'So you're as fast as they say,' Conn rasped.

'And you're too handy with a knife.' McCabe's eyes were cold and watchful. 'Turn around and I'll draw your fangs.' He waited until Conn had complied, then jerked the long-bladed knife from the sheath resting between the big man's shoulder-blades. He sensed Conn's tension, and warned. 'Try something, if you fancy your chance, but you'll collect a slug if you do.'

'I ain't gonna raise hell with you.' Conn spoke huskily. 'I got more sense.'

'So what was the last job you did for Thorn? It was last night, huh?' McCabe stepped around Conn until he could look into the man's fleshy, glowering face. 'I saw you last night giving a message to Rosie Dean. You told her Thorn wanted to see her in his hotel room about ten.'

'So?'

'So she ain't been seen since, and Billy was found dead this morning, knifed in the back. Come to think of it, you have a lot of explaining to do. The sheriff will be interested in checking your knife. Let's go, Conn. You know the way to the law office.'

The big man looked as if he wanted to protest, but the menace of McCabe's steady sixgun convinced him that he had better obey orders. He walked to the door, and McCabe called to the storeman.

'I'll collect my order shortly,' he said. 'Have it ready when I get back.'

Conn's boots hit the sidewalk with a hollow thump, and then he twisted like a cat, amazingly fast, and almost took McCabe by surprise. But McCabe's reflexes were hair-triggered, and he lifted his gun and crashed the long barrel against Conn's right temple, aiming for the spot just below the man's hatbrim. There was a sickening thud as the weapon made contact.

Conn dropped to his knees as his legs buckled, but reached out both powerful hands towards McCabe, who slammed his muzzle against the line of Conn's jaw. The big man groaned and collapsed to the sidewalk. McCabe stood over him, ready to deal out more punishment, but Conn was unconscious.

'What's going on?' Sheriff Sarran was coming along the sidewalk, and McCabe looked up, his face set in grim lines.

'Conn doesn't like the idea of Thorn being behind bars,' he said, thumbing back his hatbrim. 'He started to pull a knife so I gave him a sedative.'

'I reckon he killed Billy.' Sarran's face turned ugly as he thought about it. 'What am I gonna do with this skunk? I told Thorn I had to kill Conn this morning, and if I wanta make hay out of that situation I'll have to keep them apart.'

'I'll leave you to deal with it.' McCabe pulled his hatbrim low over his eyes. 'I need to hit the trail. Time is wasting. See you when I get back.'

Sarran nodded, his attention on the big, inert figure of Blade Conn. McCabe turned and went back into the store, and the storeman grinned in relief, pausing to wipe his forehead with a large handkerchief.

'That was one heap of trouble,' he said.

'Conn's sleeping now,' McCabe said. 'You got anything to add to what you were saying earlier about Al Spooner? Who was the bad company he was mixing with?'

The storeman sighed. 'I got nothing

more to say. It ain't safe around here to give an opinion. Here's your order.' He lifted a gunny-sack on to the counter.

McCabe paid for the supplies and left the store, his eyes narrowed as he looked around the wide, sunlit street. He saw his horse, ready saddled, standing hip-shot at the hitching rail outside the Wells Fargo office. Two men dressed in range garb were standing on the sidewalk in front of the nearby saloon, and another man was watering his horse at the trough in front of the livery barn some fifty yards along the street.

McCabe went towards the Wells Fargo office, his mind busy on the situation. But he was intent only on riding out and picking up tracks of the Gotch gang. He reached his horse and put the sack of supplies behind the cantle, tying it in place with a couple of saddle thongs. His gaze kept flitting around the street as he instinctively checked his surroundings.

He saw the man watering his horse

in front of the stable pull a rifle from its saddle holster and his teeth clicked together. Dropping his right hand to his gun, his gaze flicked back to the two men nearby on the sidewalk, and he dropped to one knee, palming his gun when he saw that they were now holding their weapons and turning towards him.

A rifle cracked flatly, the raucous sound killing the silence, and a slug splattered against a post a scant inch from McCabe's head. He ignored it, his attention on the two men in front of him. One was in the act of aiming at him, and McCabe threw up his gun and fired without seeming to aim. The weapon blasted, throwing a string of echoes across the town, and the man instantly sagged to the boards and lay writhing. The second man dropped to one knee, lifting his gun, and McCabe fired twice, eyes slitted and the acrid taste of gunsmoke in his teeth. He saw the man sprawl over sideways and lie still.

Willard Harpley appeared in the doorway of the Wells Fargo office, and McCabe yelled at him in warning, twisting to get a sight of the third man in front of the barn. The rifle cracked again and McCabe felt a burning sensation across the top of his left shoulder. He triggered his gun twice, long shots for a Colt, and got to his feet as the man staggered and then dropped lifelessly into the thick dust.

The echoes were fading sullenly as Harpley came to McCabe's side. There was a gun in the Wells Fargo manager's hand, and he looked at McCabe questioningly, his face taut with shock. McCabe shook his head. He reloaded the spent chambers in his gun as he looked around, ready for more trouble.

'I don't know who they are or what it's about.' he said tightly, answering Harpley's unspoken questions. 'But I sure as hell want to find out. There's too much back-shooting around here, and the local law needs tightening up.

I figure we got a right to do what we can about it if the sheriff ain't pulling his weight.'

'Let's make a start with these three guys,' Harpley replied grimly. 'But I don't hold out much hope with them, the way you handle things. I reckon you've killed them.'

'I didn't have time to try and wing them. The chips were down,' McCabe replied grimly. He checked the cylinder of his Colt, closed the weapon, and held it ready for more trouble as he walked towards the two men lying on the sidewalk.

6

McCabe stood motionless, watching his surroundings while Harpley bent to check the two men lying on the sidewalk. McCabe's ears were ringing from the quick blasts of the shooting, and he holstered his gun and watched the townsfolk appearing as if from nowhere to come running to see what had happened. Sarran was along the street, and for a few moments the sheriff seemed to have no idea what to do. Finally he came at a run towards the Wells Fargo office.

Harpley straightened. His face was set in grim lines, his eyes filled with bleakness. 'They're both dead,' he said harshly. 'One is a stranger. I ain't seen him around town before. But the other is a wanted man. I know his face from somewhere.'

McCabe gazed down at the sprawled

bodies. He nodded. 'Yeah, I know of this one. He's Hank Petch,' he said slowly. 'I've seen his picture on a poster. He's a badman right enough. But this other guy is a stranger to me.'

'Let's take a look at the guy down at the stable,' Harpley said. 'They sure meant to nail you, McCabe, huh?'

At that moment the sheriff arrived, breathless and shocked. He stared at the dead men for what seemed an interminable time before lifting his gaze to McCabe's implacable face.

'You're a corpse-maker, McCabe,' he accused. 'You kill men like I'd snuff out a candle.' He shook his head slowly. 'These must be more of Sam Gotch's gang, huh? And they were laying for you right here in town. What in hell is going on? It seems everyone and his uncle are after you, and you walk untouched through everything that's thrown at you!'

'This one is Hank Petch,' McCabe responded, toeing the dead man in question. 'He's wanted by the law for murder and robbery. Check out your dodgers, Sheriff, and you'll mebbe find him. But I ain't heard that he's running with Gotch.' He turned and pushed through the growing crowd of townsmen and went to his horse. Harpley accompanied him, and McCabe led his horse along the street to the stable, where the third man in the ambush was lying. He glanced back over his shoulder once to see Sarran giving orders to the townsmen.

'You figure Sarran ain't doing his job properly?' Harpley demanded.

'It sure looks that way to me.' McCabe shrugged. 'But it's none of my business. I've got my job to do and I need to get on with it. But so far I've been caught up in events that don't seem to concern me, unless they are connected with Sam Gotch. That's why I've got to check out everything happening around here.'

He trailed his reins when they reached the man sprawled beside the water trough and his eyes were slitted. He was bleak inside. The ambush had been a near thing. He looked down at the man and saw that he was dead, with two splotches of blood on his shirt front barely an inch apart. He was unknown to McCabe, who shook his head silently.

'That was mighty fine shooting from back there,' Harpley acknowledged admiringly.

'No. One shot would have done.' McCabe spoke grimly. 'I must be getting nervous.' He glanced around before turning his attention to the dead man, and spotted the stableman standing just inside the big doorway of the barn, peering out at the street. 'Did you see these three come into town?' he called, and the man emerged and came hesitantly to the trough.

'This feller rode in about five minutes before the shooting started. He was standing here at the trough, letting his horse drink, until he pulled his rifle and tried to shoot you. The other two put their horses in the barn about thirty minutes ago. I didn't like the look of them so I kept an eye on them. I sure didn't think they were laying for you. I didn't get time even to shout when the shooting started.'

McCabe nodded. He studied the dead man's inert face and shook his head. 'I'm certain I never saw him before,' he said. 'What about you, Harpley?'

'Nope.' The Wells Fargo man shook his head.

'So what about their horses?' McCabe turned his attention to the horse standing nearby with trailing reins. He walked around it, looking for a brand, and shook his head for the animal was unbranded.

'I've seen this animal in here several times,' the stableman said eagerly. 'This guy works for Joel Slater out at the JS ranch, I reckon. He's come into town more than once with some of Joel Slater's crew.'

'That's worth knowing.' McCabe

nodded. 'What about the broncs those other two rode?'

They entered the barn and the stableman led the way to a stall where two horses were tethered.

'The black was ridden in by the guy wearing the red shirt,' he announced.

'That was Petch.' McCabe checked the animal. 'No brand,' he observed. The horse was a big animal, bred for speed and stamina, and that figured for a man with a price on his head. The second horse was likewise unbranded. 'Did you get a good look at the two men when they brought their horses in here?' he asked the stableman.

'Sure did, and the sight of them worried me. But I haven't seen either of them before.'

'Well we've got one of them tied in with JS,' Harpley mused. 'And we're gonna have some trouble with Joel Slater in the near future, McCabe. He's squatting on water that belongs to Wells Fargo. I figure Frank Holbrooke is coming in here to get things moving where Slater is concerned.'

'Slater seemed to be real friendly with the sheriff when I rode in yesterday,' McCabe mused. 'What about Slater? What kind of a man is he?'

'He's been complaining of trouble with rustlers.' Harpley grimaced. 'But he's got a tough crew out at JS. I reckon he could handle anything a bunch of rustlers threw at him. Mebbe he's just making smoke around his own actions, huh?'

'I'm riding out,' McCabe decided. 'If I stick around I might never get the chance to do what I came for. Keep an eye open around here, Harpley. And when I get back you can let me know what happened in my absence. I've got to get on Gotch's trail before it turns cold.'

He left the stable then, determined to get to grips with his real job. Harpley accompanied him, and McCabe gathered up his reins and swung into his saddle. He lifted a hand to Harpley and touched spurs to his horse, and as he cantered clear of town he heaved a long sigh of relief.

He had become too involved in what had happened in town. He needed to get to grips with Sam Gotch, and afterwards, if he was still alive, he could turn his attention to those other matters. He grimaced as he thought of young Billy Dean, and wondered what had happened to Rosie Dean. When he thought of Al Spooner, the chief deputy, and what the man had tried to do, he shook his head and stifled his thoughts, for he could gain no clear picture of anything.

He looked around to get his bearings and headed back along the trail, making for the scene of yesterday's hold-up. This business seemed to be the most complicated he had ever handled, and he wondered why Frank Holbrooke had revealed his identity to just about everyone in town? It didn't add up. Frank believed in giving his operatives all the facts. But there seemed to be something missing from the general briefing, and McCabe racked his brains in trying to get some of the questions and answers facing him to match up.

When he reached the area where Gotch and his bunch had attacked the coach after the attempted hold-up, McCabe rode slowly, studying the hard trail for signs of the attack. Presently he saw a body sprawled in long grass beside the trail, and reined in to look around before dismounting. His face was set in harsh lines when he turned over the crumpled figure and looked into a bearded face that was frozen in death. There was a big bloodstain on the man's chest, and McCabe pictured the scene of the previous afternoon, when he had shot at the outlaws pursuing the coach. This man had been wearing a gunny-sack when he fell out of his saddle, and McCabe looked around for it in vain.

He hunkered down and studied sign. Someone had dragged the dead man off the trail and then searched the body. The dead man's pockets had been turned inside out. There were footprints in the surrounding dust, and he followed them several yards until he came to a spot where a horse had waited. The rider had headed south after leaving the body, taking the dead man's horse with him. McCabe tried to recall details of the outlaw's horse but had been too busily engaged at the time to be able to note anything.

He continued, leaving the body where it lay. He checked out the tracks of other horses that had been made within the last twenty-four hours, but found nothing about them to remember for future reference. Three sets of tracks had branched from the trail about the spot where Gotch and the rest of his bunch had given up the chase, and McCabe decided to track them, remembering that one of the three riders, Rattlesnake Riley, had been in town at ten o'clock the previous evening.

He recalled details of the map of the county he had studied in the sheriff's office, and figured he had a good grasp on the whereabouts of most of the cattle spreads in the area. Now he needed some luck. He wanted to run Sam Gotch to earth.

The three sets of prints led him to the south-east, and separated in rough ground about ten miles from where the hold-up had taken place. One set of tracks headed north straight as a beeline, and the others turned south, striking into even rougher country.

McCabe figured the prints going north alone belonged to Rattlesnake Riley on his way to town, and he turned south, his keen gaze on the faint prints as he followed them. He needed to know where they finished up, and had to use all his patience to remain alert as he followed steadily.

He had travelled fifteen miles from the spot where he had seen the dead man when the tracks disappeared in an outcrop of rock. Dismounting to give his horse a breather, he dropped to one knee to check the ground, and nodded when he spotted signs that the tracks had been blotted out by someone good at the job.

McCabe checked his surroundings. He had to be close to the JS ranch now, he figured. Joel Slater's spread. And Slater had employed one of the three men in town who had tried to kill McCabe that morning. But Slater was not his business at the moment, unless Sam Gotch had ridden into the JS ranch.

The sun was well over into the western half of the sky, and McCabe trailed his reins, permitting the horse to move slowly through the rocks grazing on what little vegetation there was. Moving out on foot, McCabe walked a hundred yards to the south and then cast around in a wide circle, using the high ground where he had lost the tracks as a pivot for his search. He found the missing tracks almost immediately, still heading south, and was pleased with himself as he walked back to fetch his horse.

Another hour's ride brought him in sight of a big ranch headquarters, and he remained in cover five hundred yards out to study it, using his field glasses. There was the glint of water to the left of the buildings and slightly beyond, and McCabe wondered if it was the creek that belonged to Wells Fargo.

He delved into his sack of provisions and ate cold food, washing it down with the tepid water in his canteen. The sun was lowering towards the distant western horizon and long shadows were beginning to creep over the heat-tortured ground. When darkness came he mounted and rode in a wide circle to approach the ranch from the east, pausing at the creek out of sight and sound of the ranch to enable his horse to drink. Then he led the animal into cover and knee-hobbled it. This was where he began earning his pay.

He drew his Winchester from its saddle scabbard and checked it, then began to walk in the direction of the ranch. The darkness was now sufficient to cloak his movements. He reached the fence surrounding the yard and eased between the poles, keeping to the shadows and making for the bunkhouse off to the left where yellow lantern light filled the windows.

The sound of a guitar being strummed filled the night with soft music. McCabe moved in behind the bunkhouse and remained motionless for long minutes, listening and checking out the area. He finally edged along one side of the bunkhouse until he reached a window, and when he peered into the interior he saw at least a dozen men inside the long, low building. Some were relaxing on their bunks. Four sat at a table, playing cards, and the man with the guitar was seated on a corner of the table.

McCabe studied faces, but none of them was known to him. He eased away and began a circuit of the yard, taking his time, and finished up behind the house. He had seen lights in the lower windows in the front of the house, and edged in closer until he was sheltering at the left side of the veranda. Studying the yard, he was aware that anyone out front would be able to spot him the moment he closed in on a lighted window for a looksee.

But he had to take the risk, and removed his spurs before movinq on to the dusty boards. He flattened himself against the front wall of the house and edged sideways until he was beside a lighted window. Easing his shoulders sideways he risked a glance into the room, and a silent sigh gusted from him when he saw three men seated around a desk. The room was obviously the ranch office, and McCabe recognized Joel Slater sitting behind the desk, talking intently, a glass of whiskey in his left hand and a cigar in his right. The room was blue with cigarette smoke, and the window, opened a crack at the top, emitted a steady flow of smoke plus the sound of Slater's rasping voice.

'I figure you better start out for town

now if you're gonna be in the right place at sun-up,' Slater was saying.

McCabe's eyes glittered when he looked at the other two men in the room and realized that one was Sam Gotch. There was no mistaking the scar adorning the left side of the gang boss's weathered face. The other man was Wiley Benns, another wanted outlaw, and McCabe clenched his hands as he figured that he was close to a showdown. But he needed to know what was going on here, and crouched a little as he eaves-dropped on the conversation.

Gotch scratched the black stubble on his heavy face. His dark eyes were narrowed, and he was shaking his head as if disagreeing with Slater.

'I can't ride into town until Riley shows up,' he snarled. 'I should've known better than to send him in alone. I figger he's hit the nearest saloon and likkered hisself up. Probably sleeping it off now, and we're waiting for him to get back with news.'

'You can't wait any longer,' Slater rasped. 'You've got to hit the bank in the morning soon as it opens. They'll be shipping the dough out before noon. Hell, I don't hafta tell you your job, do I? If you don't see Riley then you'll have to see Dave Thorn yourself. You've got to hit the bank in the morning. There won't be that much dough in the place again for months.'

'How can you be sure?' Gotch shook his head. 'You said you spoke to that sidewinder Sarran in town a couple of days ago, but I figger he's all snake. You can't never trust a lawman. He's mebbe waiting with a posse for me to ride into town to grab me for the price on my head.'

'He's got more to gain by stringing along with us,' Slater insisted. 'Sarran's got to do what I tell him. I got the deadwood on him, I can tell you.'

'Well I don't like it.' Gotch gently rubbed his scar where it curved down towards his mouth. It was white and jagged, and looked ghastly in the lamplight. 'Thorn is too big for his boots. He figgers he's got a right to the Dean spread. I told you before, Slater, that you should put a slug in Thorn. There ain't no place for him in our kind've set-up. He's playing for big stakes, and he wants it all for hisself.'

'I'll kill him soon as he stops being useful,' Slater said grimly. 'You worry too much, Sam.' He laughed harshly, his eyes narrowing. 'I keep telling you there ain't nothing going to spoil what we've got going.'

'No?' Wiley Benns pushed back his thin shoulders. His gaunt face, with its sunken cheeks and pale complexion, would have looked bad on a corpse, McCabe figured. Benns stifled a racking cough and reached for the whiskey bottle on the desk, splashing rotgut carelessly into his glass and over the papers strewn on the desk. 'You saw what McCabe did to us at the hold-up, Sam. I figure the smart thing to do is pull out until things settle down again. Wells Fargo will make a big thing of hunting us down, and McCabe is one of those guys who can't be killed. I've told you what I heard about him. He was outside the law for years, a killer down in the south-west. If you don't put him down then we gotta move out. It's as simple as that.'

'Forget about McCabe.' Slater's pale eyes glittered in the lamplight. 'I figured he was a bad threat soon as I clapped eyes on him in town, and I sent three men in to take care of him this morning. They probably got him buried on Boot Hill now, so you could be worrying about nothing. Ride into town and check out the situation, Sam. Thorn will give you the latest dope, and when you get the dough tomorrow hightail it to my line cabin on the north boundary and lay low until I send you word the heat is off.'

Gotch lumbered to his feet, shaking his head. 'I disagree with Benns, but I got a bad feeling about this anyway,' he grated. 'We should have taken that coach easy, but where in hell did

McCabe come from, and how did he know we were waiting there to hit the coach at that time? I tell you, Slater, you're not the only one getting information. McCabe is hell on wheels with a gun, and he sure turned up like he knew what was about to happen. I reckon there's no telling what he's been doing in town since he showed up there. He might have put the deadwood on the whole deal by now, and I'd be a prize sucker to ride in there into a trap.'

'You're getting mighty nervous in your old age,' Slater jeered. 'You'll be running from shadows next. One man turns up and your gang has gone to pieces.'

'Cole McCabe is a one-man army,' Wiley Benns said sharply. 'I tell you, Sam, we got to put McCabe down before he hits us again. Taking care of him's got to be the first thing we do or you can forget about the easy pickings around here.'

'We're riding to town now,' Gotch

said heavily, 'and if McCabe ain't dead already then we'll take care of him. Will that satisfy you, Slater?'

'You know how to handle the deal,' Slater replied, grinning. 'You better take Blackie Tobin and Rafe Carter outa the bunkhouse to side you. Two of you can't handle that chore in town tomorrow. Do it right and nobody will have any complaints.'

McCabe eased back into the gloom as Gotch and Benns left the office. His mind was reeling under the impact of what he had overheard. It seemed that everyone in town of any consequence was working with the outlaws. He departed silently, keeping to the shadows, eager now to get back to his horse and trail Gotch to town.

He sneaked back around the bunk-house and moved in again to look through a window. Gotch appeared in the doorway of the bunkhouse and the guitarist stopped playing as all eyes turned towards his big figure.

Grinning, Gotch stroked the scar on his left cheek.

'Tobin and Carter,' he called. 'You're riding into town with me.'

Two men moved forward. One was tall and heavily built, with dark eyes and black hair. His large face was almost invisible under a shaggy black beard. The second man was small, medium-sized, with yellow hair and a narrow face, and when he smiled he reminded McCabe of a rat.

'You got something doin'?' the big man asked.

'Slater said you two can be trusted to keep your mouths shut,' Gotch responded. 'So don't ask questions. I'll tell you anything you need to know when I think the time is right. Go saddle up. Benns is at the corral. Wait with him until I show.'

The two men collected their gear and moved out. Gotch looked around the silent ranch hands for a moment, then turned on his heel and departed. McCabe left the window and eased back into the shadows. He walked silently back to where he had left his horse, readied it for the trail, checked his sixgun, and was mounted and waiting when four horsemen passed him by within twenty yards of his position.

They were riding towards the far-off town, and McCabe fell in behind them at a distance of one hundred yards, unable to see them but following them by sound, the sounds of his own horse blotted out by the noise made by the four horses ahead.

Wary of the dangerous chore he was pursuing, McCabe halted many times to listen to his prey riding steadily towards town. He had instinctively decided against bracing the four men before reaching town because he would not have an edge in the night. If shooting broke out he would be at a severe disadvantage, and he needed to fight from a position of strength.

While he rode McCabe considered the information he had gleaned from

Joel Slater. He was shocked by the proof that the sheriff was one of the renegades. He needed the strength of the local law to support him, and would have to change his tactics considerably. Sarran had to be arrested before the situation progressed to its climax.

He was uncertain about trusting anyone in town. Who had given Gotch his information about Wells Fargo shipments? The sheriff would not have had access to it. Someone working for Wells Fargo must have passed it on, and only Willard Harpley would be in a position to do that, so was he guilty of betraying his employers?

McCabe puzzled over the scraps of information whirling around in his teeming mind. He needed everything to fit together before starting his clean-up. When the shooting began he wanted to be sure of his actions or innocent people might get killed. And he wanted to catch everyone connected with the outlaws, dead or alive.

He was so wrapped up with his

conflicting thoughts that it was some time before he suddenly became aware that he was being followed. He was straining his ears to pick up the sounds of the four men ahead of him, but several times a slight sound to his rear had reached him — the click of a hoof against a stone, the creak of leather — and he had not been alerted. When realization finally came his hair lifted on the back of his neck and he drew his gun, instantly prepared to sell his life dearly as the follower drew nearer.

7

McCabe sat motionless in the shadows, a cold sensation between his shoulder-blades as he listened to the nearing sounds reaching his ears from behind. Now that he was aware of them they were so loud he wondered who could be foolish enough to trail him this close. Had there been a guard at Slater's place who picked up his presence? He discounted that thought. If he had been seen he would not have got this far.

The four riders ahead were moving at a canter, as they had ever since leaving the JS, and they soon passed out of the range of McCabe's hearing. They ascended a steep incline in the trail and were quickly gone. McCabe held his reins in his left hand and his gun in his right as he faced his rear. His gun was steady as he tensely waited for his tracker to come up with him. Then the faint shape of a rider slowly materialized out of the shadows and McCabe lifted his gun, his finger trembling on the trigger.

He did not want to shoot and alert Gotch to his presence, and held his fire as the rider approached. The newcomer was a shapeless mass and McCabe watched for any quick movement that would warn of impending action. But the rider came on steadily, and McCabe soon saw that the man's right hand was held upraised in the sign of peace.

'Cole, this is Frank Holbrooke,' the man called in a harsh undertone. 'I was wondering when you'd pick me up. I been making noise to attract you but you sure took your time getting around to me. If I'd been Sam Gotch you'd be dead by now. Are you getting careless in your old age?'

'Frank!' McCabe was stunned by the revelation. 'What in hell are you doing here? Harpley has been expecting you to show up in town. How did you get on to me?'

'I've been watching the comings and goings at JS for a couple of days now, and I recognized you when you looked through the window of Slater's office. I was at the opposite corner of the porch and saw your face in the light of the window. It didn't take you long to drop on to Gotch. He's been using the ranch as a hideout and working hand in glove with Slater. Did you hear enough to work out what's been going on around here?'

'Can we keep riding on Gotch's trail?' McCabe asked. 'He's on his way to hit the bank first thing in the morning.'

'Sure he is. I played for him to do just that. I arranged for some false information to be fed to Slater about a money shipment, and I planned to drop on to you in town before dawn to alert you. I figured that between us we could take care of Gotch and his bunch when the chips were down.'

'You've been holding out on me, Frank,' McCabe accused. He turned his head and listened for sounds of his quarry, but heard only the wind sighing in his ears and knew the outlaws had pulled well ahead. He sighed and relaxed. 'But you played a mighty dangerous game, sneaking up behind me in the night when I was keyed up about Gotch.'

'We all have to take risks at times.' Holbrooke laughed softly. 'You did real good, Cole. You mebbe got a mite snarled up in town with some of the side stuff going on there. But I needed you in there without your usual cover story because I knew you'd stir things up and mebbe force a few more of the badmen to show their hands. You sure got out here faster than I figured you would. You've learned a whole lot about our business in the last two years, huh?'

'There was a murder in town that might have been avoided if I hadn't gone in like a bull,' McCabe said bitterly.

'Murder?' Holbrooke dismounted and

trailed his reins and McCabe followed suit. They faced each other in the shadows, unable to see more than their bare outlines.

'Young Billy Dean.' McCabe gave a brief account of what had occurred in town, adding that Rosie had gone missing.

'Harpley told me about the Deans a year ago.' Holbrooke took his canteen from the saddle horn and there was a gurgling sound as he drank sparingly. 'I figured Billy and his sister got a raw deal when their pa was killed. Dave Thorn sewed up his crooked business all ways to the middle. Art Pell, the lawyer, and Ash Tolliver, the banker, were in on that deal, and I know about it because I had already learned that Tolliver has been milking the Wells Fargo account while Pell falsifies the figures. There's gonna be a reckoning with that pair before long.' He paused and heaved a sigh. 'I hoped to clean up in town before anything bad happened to the Deans. So Billy was killed and

Rosie disappeared, huh? Young Billy was earmarked for a job like yours when he grew big enough. He hated killers, Cole, and I figured that in about five years he would have sided you. What a pair you two would have made.'

'I got Thorn and Rattlesnake Riley in jail,' McCabe cut in. 'But if Sarran is crooked then that won't mean a thing, huh?'

'You're damn right. I reckon they walked free the minute your back was turned. Now listen, Cole. You got a few things to do before dawn, mighty important things. Forget about Gotch for now. I know where he will be at nine-thirty in the morning. Ride into town and contact Harpley. Tell him I got it set up like we planned, and that's all you'll tell him. Keep the rest of this to yourself.'

'Don't you trust Harpley? I was wondering where Gotch was getting the inside information from. Harpley was the only man with that knowledge.'

'I had a hand in that, Cole. I figure that's why Billy Dean was killed. The boy was working for me. I had to take advantage of his hatred for Dave Thorn and his desire to work permanently for Wells Fargo, and it worked a treat. Billy got the information out of Harpley's safe and passed it on to Thorn because I told him it would trap those men who were responsible for his father's death. Gotch hit some small shipments of money as a result, and fell into the trap when Billy passed on false word about the biggest shipment ever. There ain't gonna be any money, but Gotch and his bunch will be right where I want them. We're heading for the showdown, Cole, but there are some weak spots in the plan that we need to strengthen before morning. I've tried to cover this trap all ways to the middle, but I got a nasty feeling that something I ain't considered might crop up and ruin it.'

McCabe shook his head, shocked by the revelations. It looked as if young

Billy Dean didn't have a chance from the beginning, a youngster thrown in amongst a bunch of wolves. And what had happened to Rosie Dean? He dragged his mind from his thoughts. Holbrooke was talking again, and he returned his attention to the situation.

'After you talk to Harpley you go to the law office and throw Sarran in his own jail, then wait in the office and arrest everyone who walks into the place. Throw 'em all in the cells and wait until Jabez Eke shows up.'

'Eke! I know that name. Ain't he an odd-job man around town? Harpley or Sarran mentioned him as a likely suspect when I said I figured someone in town was passing information to Gotch.'

'Yeah. I told Eke to play it tough when I sent him in undercover, and even Harpley isn't aware that he's one of my men. I've had him in town for some weeks, watching points and keeping me informed.'

'So that's howcome you know so

much.' McCabe grinned, filled with admiration. Then he shook his head. 'I figure you could have made my job that much easier by telling me everything, Frank. I had to start out suspecting everyone. Working in the dark made my side of it that much harder.'

'That's right. I wanted you to act naturally, and mebbe you couldn't have done that had you known everything. There are still one or two badmen in town who have covered their tracks real well, and I need to smoke them out into the open before I finish the whole business. When you arrest Sarran and jug him there'll be some in town who'll have to do something about that, and you could be knee-deep in trouble. Now get this straight, Cole. When Eke shows up you hand over to him. He'll be working to a timetable so don't waste a minute. Leave the jail immediately and head for the lawyer's home. Art Pell has reached the end of his rope and you can pick him up and jail him. Gotch and the men with him will be hiding out in the bank by that time, with Ash Tolliver's connivance, waiting for the alleged money shipment to arrive from Dodge City around nine-thirty. I'll have the place surrounded by six picked men who will have arrived in town on the dawn stage.'

'So this is a big operation,' McCabe mused. 'And you brought me in at the end of it when I figured it was just the start.'

'You were busy elsewhere when it started.' Holbrooke swung back into his saddle. 'I still got a lot of riding to do before the sun comes up.'

'What do I do after Pell's been jailed?' McCabe demanded. 'I like to know my part several moves ahead, Frank.'

'Stay with Eke in the jail. You should get callers who need to talk to Sarran about what's happening, and anyone who walks into the jail gets put behind bars until I can check them out.'

'And when Gotch hits the bank?'

'You stay out of it, Cole. I got

that worked out. Soon as the Gotch bunch is settled I'll wanta check on who you've arrested. I figure there will be some surprises, but that's the way it goes in this business.'

'Is that all I got to do?' McCabe was disappointed and it sounded in his voice. He had been looking forward to bracing the Gotch gang alone, in the way that he usually worked. But he knew Holbrooke well enough to obey orders without question.

'Your side of it is most important,' Holbrooke said. His head and shoulders were silhouetted against the night sky, and saddle leather creaked as he swung his horse around. 'Don't crowd Gotch and those others on the way into town, Cole. I don't want them getting skittish. You do just like I say, and I'll see you at the jail when it's all over.'

McCabe did not reply, and Holbrooke touched spurs to his horse and vanished into the night, going back in the direction he had arrived. The sound of hooves echoed for a moment, then stillness resumed, and McCabe heaved a long sigh as he climbed into his saddle and continued to town, his mind buzzing with what he had learned from the chief detective.

Following the faint trail, McCabe rode at a canter, filled with disappointment by the small part he had been allotted to play in the coming fight with the outlaws. He had been keyed up for a bone with meat on it but Holbrooke had tossed him scraps, and it stuck in his craw.

He figured that the Gotch bunch were at least a mile ahead but did not relax his vigilance. The night was not real dark to eyes accustomed to the shadows and he constantly checked his surroundings as he rode. The thud of his mount's hooves formed a dull background to the darkness, and did not blot out the sound of the single shot that suddenly hammered and echoed.

McCabe reined in and sat listening intently. The shot had come from way ahead and he wondered at its significance. Echoes were reverberating slowly and he waited until they had faded into nothing before touching spurs to his mount and going on at a slower pace. Now his thoughts were stilled and he was at full alertness, having no desire to ride into trouble at this important stage of Frank Holbrooke's plan.

When he spotted a horse sprawled motionless on the trail he slowed to a walk, his right hand on the butt of his gun as he closed in. His narrowed eyes searched for the more ominous shape of a man, but he saw nothing, and reined in and stepped down from his saddle. The fallen horse was dead, shot through the brain, and McCabe sat back on his heels for a moment when he'd ascertained that the animal had broken a foreleg.

Was one of the horses in Gotch's bunch now carrying double or was the man afoot somewhere in the vicinity, hoping to pick up another mount? McCabe looked around through slitted eyes, and when he saw a dim light about a hundred yards off to the left of the trail he swung his horse in that direction and rode towards it. If one of Gotch's men was afoot then he had to be accounted for.

The night seemed blacker now, the trail rough and tiring. McCabe slowed his pace as he approached the small oblong of yellow light and reined in out of earshot. A shaft of light split the darkness as a door creaked open and a man emerged. McCabe was walking towards the two-storey building, and paused, hand on gun, until the door slammed and the night closed in once more. The man went off to the left towards a barn and a corral that McCabe saw only by squinting his eyes.

At that moment a woman screamed sobbingly, and McCabe froze. He was a couple of yards from the right front corner of the building, and heard the man curse and come back to the building. When the door opened,

McCabe moved in swiftly, and was only a pace behind the man as he crossed the threshold. His Colt .45 leaped into his right hand when he saw that the man in front was holding a weapon, and he jabbed his muzzle against the man's spine.

'Just stand quiet until I get the straight of what's going on here,' McCabe rasped, and the man froze in mid-stride, his hands lifting instantly. McCabe reached out with his left hand and took the pistol from the man's hand. 'I heard a woman scream, so stand still until I tell you to move. I recognize you, anyhow. You're one of the Sam Gotch gang.'

The man stood with his hands raised, not moving a muscle. McCabe could see that he was bearded, and realized it was the man whom Gotch fetched from the bunkhouse at JS.

'You're Blackie Tobin,' McCabe continued.

'Yeah, and what's it to you?' came the harsh reply.

McCabe did not answer. He glanced around the room. A man was sprawled on the floor with a woman kneeling beside him. The woman was sobbing, hands pressed to her face. There was a pool of blood around the man's head.

'Is it your horse dead on the trail?' McCabe demanded.

'Yeah. Put a foot in a hole and broke its fool leg. I came here for a fresh mount and Ellwood there decided I couldn't have one.'

'So you knifed him.' McCabe could see that the dead man's throat had been cut. 'Cold-blooded murder.'

'Who are you?' Tobin demanded, half turning around to face McCabe. 'You ain't the law!'

McCabe struck with the barrel of his gun, slamming the muzzle against the side of the man's hat. Tobin staggered, but his hat saved him from the full effect of the blow, and McCabe struck again, aiming for the right temple. There was a meaty thud and Tobin fell to the floor and lay still. McCabe stepped over him and went to the woman's side. He grimaced as he looked down at the dead man, for there was nothing he could do and he had to push on to town.

'Anything I can do to help you, ma'am?' he demanded. 'I'm on my way to Hickory. Do you wanta ride in with me?'

The woman stirred and looked up at him, her face soaked with tears, her eyes wild and staring in shock. McCabe tightened his lips, for once at a loss how to cope with a situation.

'There ain't anyone in town can help me,' the woman said in a shrill tone. 'The sheriff won't lift a hand to help. He's been pestering us over the past months, trying to get us to sell out. But Pete wouldn't, and they've been giving us hell ever since.' She got to her feet suddenly and lurched by McCabe, pausing beside the unconscious Tobin and bending to search him. 'Where's the knife he killed Pete with?' she

172

demanded. 'I'll carve Pete's name on his heart.'

McCabe dived forward to grab the woman and grasped her wrist as she pulled a hunting knife from a sheath on Tobin's belt. He disarmed her and she returned to her dead husband's side, her body racked with sobs.

'I'll take Tobin into town with me,' McCabe decided. 'He'll be in jail. I'll get someone to come out here to you, ma'am. Can I borrow a horse for Tobin to ride?'

The woman did not reply, and McCabe turned his attention to Tobin. He removed the man's gun-belt and searched him for other weapons, then bound his hands behind him with a leather thong taken from his holster. He dragged Tobin out of the house and then bound his ankles together with his gun-belt. Going to the barn, he struck a match and lit a lantern. He took a horse from the corral and saddled it.

Tobin had regained consciousness

when McCabe went back to him. McCabe removed the belt from Tobin's ankles and dragged the man upright.

'I'm taking you into town to jail,' McCabe told him.

'Sure.' Tobin laughed gratingly. 'I was heading for town anyway.'

'Yeah, in the company of Sam Gotch, the outlaw. I figure your riding days are over, Tobin.'

The man cursed McCabe, who silenced him with a blow.

'I don't wanta hear a single word out of you between here and town,' McCabe told him. He thrust Tobin into the saddle and led the animal to where his own horse was tethered, then set out for Hickory . . .

When the rising sun killed the shadows and tinged the eastern sky with crimson, McCabe eased his aching body in the saddle and forced his mind to full alertness. His prisoner was slumped in his saddle, chin on his chest, apparently sleeping. He reined up on high ground and sighed with relief when he spotted the sprawl of the town just ahead. There was no sign of Gotch and the rest of his crooked sidekicks, and McCabe wondered where they had sought cover. He circled the town and entered the livery barn.

Dragging Tobin out of his saddle, McCabe took care of both horses, and then marched Tobin out to the back lots and went in search of Willard Harpley.

Recalling Rana Harpley's directions for finding their house when she invited him to have supper with them, McCabe entered North Street and skulked through the decreasing shadows to a large, white-painted house almost on the junction with East Street.

Tobin began dragging his feet, and McCabe drew his gun and thrust the muzzle against the man's temple.

'I'll let sunlight into your skull if you give me trouble,' he said. 'Keep moving, and don't make a noise.'

Easing around to the rear of the house, McCabe saw lamplight in the kitchen and rapped softly on the door, which was opened by Willard Harpley.

The Wells Fargo manager was already dressed for the office, but he looked tired, a worried man with a load of troubles on his mind. He smiled, however, when he saw McCabe, and opened the door wide. Then he saw Tobin and a frown replaced his smile.

'Cole. I didn't expect to see you this soon. Did you have any success? This is Blackie Tobin, one of Joel Slater's men.'

'That's right. He murdered Pete Ellwood for a horse. I'm taking him to jail. I saw Frank Holbrooke on the trail and he said to tell you everything is going according to plan.'

'Frank?' Harpley shook his head. 'I'd like to know where he gets his information from.'

'You and me both.' McCabe turned away. 'I have to get moving. I've got things to do.'

'Anything I can help you with?'

'Nope. You've got your word. You

know what to do now?'

'Sure.' Harpley nodded worriedly. 'But the trouble with Holbrooke is that he never tells you more than he has to, and that makes a man worry about what is going on around him. Where will you be in case I should need you quickly.'

McCabe turned away, his left hand grasping Tobin's thick shoulder. 'I can't tell you,' he said. 'See you later.'

He escorted Tobin to the main street and turned right, keeping on the sidewalk and close to the buildings. The law office was a couple of blocks ahead, and McCabe narrowed his eyes when he saw a saddle horse hitched to the rail in front of the building. He closed on the office and then dragged Tobin into an alley and waited, his impatience growing as minutes slipped by and the early morning was imperceptibly brightened by the rising sun.

A rider came into town from the north and went by steadily, apparently heading for the stable. McCabe grimaced. He had to make his move. He pushed Tobin out of the alley mouth and covered the last yards to the law office. As he reached the door it was opened and Sheriff Sarran appeared. The lawman halted in his tracks, his face expressing surprise.

'Heck, I didn't expect you back for a couple of days at least,' he jerked out. 'Have you got a line of Gotch?'

'Sure.' McCabe smiled. 'Let's go inside and I'll tell you about it. You know this man, huh?'

'Yeah. Blackie Tobin. Rides for Joel Slater. What's he doing with his hands tied?'

McCabe pushed Tobin, forward and followed, forcing the sheriff to move backwards. McCabe entered the office and closed the door at his back, his keen gaze never leaving Sarran's face. With a quick movement he drew his sixgun, and the three clicks as he cocked it sounded inordinately loud in the early morning. Sarran looked down at the weapon in disbelief and instinctively lifted his hands.

'What this?' he demanded. 'Have you gone loco?'

'Just obeying orders,' McCabe rasped. He snaked Sarran's pistol out of its holster and stuck it into the waistband of his pants. 'Where are your jail keys? I got to put you behind bars.'

'Me? What in hell for?' Sarran bristled. 'You got no right to come in here like this.'

McCabe waggled his gun, smiling grimly. 'This is all the right I need,' he said. 'Are my other prisoners locked up?'

Sarran's expression hardened. 'They ain't,' he said. 'A hardcase walked in after midnight with a gun in his hand and turned them loose. I was held until they cleared out of town.'

'And what have you done about it?' McCabe demanded. 'Did you let Harpley know?'

'I ain't done a thing about it yet.' Sarran shook his head. 'There was nothing I could do until sun-up.'

'Forget about it now and head for the cells. I got to put you under lock and key until further orders. You'll have Tobin to keep you company.'

'Whose orders?' Sarran demanded. 'There'll be hell to pay over this.'

'That ain't none of my concern. I'm only doing my job.' McCabe saw a bunch of keys lying on the sheriff's desk and picked them up. He motioned with his gun to the thick wooden door in the wall at the rear of the office. 'The cells are through there, huh? Lead the way and we'll get this done.'

Sarran realized that it was useless to argue, and shrugged fatalistically as he turned to obey. He opened the door and went into the cell block, followed by a grim-faced Tobin. McCabe followed closely, and shook his head when he saw that all the cells were unoccupied. He locked Sarran and Tobin in adjoining cells and returned to the outer office, ignoring the questions Sarran threw at him.

Locking the connecting door, McCabe

threw the bunch of keys on the desk and sank tiredly into the seat behind it. Weariness was crawling through him but he fought it off, and at that moment the street door was thrust open and Blade Conn stepped into the office. McCabe tensed. His job now was to arrest and jail everyone who visited Sarran before Jabez Eke arrived, and he was gratified that his first visitor was one of the men who had been turned loose during the night.

8

McCabe got to his feet, his hand dropping to the butt of his holstered gun. 'Welcome back,' he greeted.

Conn paused in surprise, gaping at McCabe as if unable to believe his eyes. Then his right hand flashed up to the back of his neck, fingers clawing out the knife sheathed at his nape. McCabe set his gunhand moving and the big weapon seemed to leap into his hand. He cocked the weapon as Conn withdrew his knife from its sheath, and the black hole of the muzzle gaped at Conn's chest. The big man stayed his movement and stood with the haft of the knife gripped in the fingers of his right hand, the deadly point of the blade still in the sheath. His expression indicated that he was hesitant about surrendering.

'Try it if you like,' McCabe said.

'I'm itching to kill you, Conn. I figure you knifed Billy Dean.'

Conn straightened slowly, letting his right hand fall to his side. The knife clattered to the floor and he kicked it aside. His fingers were dangerously close to the gun holstered on his right hip but he knew better than to try for the weapon while McCabe had him covered.

'I didn't kill that youngster,' Conn snarled. 'What are you trying to pull?'

'Who busted you out of jail?' McCabe countered.

'What's it to you, huh? Are you a lawman?' Conn's face took on a hard expression and his fierce eyes glittered.

'Get your hands up.' McCabe waggled his gun. 'I'm looking for a chance to plug you.' He waited for the man to obey. 'Now turn around.'

Conn moved reluctantly, and McCabe stepped in close and pulled the man's gun from its holster. Conn came whirling around as the weapon rasped clear of leather, his hands lifting to grasp at McCabe, who moved backwards half a pace. McCabe's pistol was already swinging in a short arc, and as Conn grabbed at him the muzzle of the weapon slammed solidly against the big man's left temple with all of McCabe's considerable weight behind it.

Conn swayed like a tree that had been hit by the blade of an axe. His hands fell away wide of his body, his eyes glazing as he pitched over backwards. He hit the floor with a crash that shook the office and lay inert, breathing heavily.

McCabe regarded him with brooding gaze. He stuck Conn's gun into his waistband against his spine and then holstered his own weapon and picked up the bunch of keys from the desk. Taking Conn by the scruff of the neck, he dragged the unconscious man into the cell block and dumped him in a cell. He locked the door before glancing at Sarran, who was sitting on the end of the bunk in his cell.

'Conn just couldn't stay away,' he observed. 'Why do you reckon he came back?'

Sarran did not reply, and McCabe retreated to the office, locking the door at his back. He sat down at the desk and tried to relax. He was tired but knew there would be no rest for him until Holbrooke finally sprang his trap. Impatience clawed at his mind. He wanted to be out there doing what he was good at instead of being tied to the office with nothing to handle.

His thoughts roved over the events that had occurred since his arrival, and a big question confronted him. What had happened to Rosie Dean? He got up and paced the office, his mind flitting over the accumulated facts of the case as he knew them. But no clues were presenting themselves as normally happened when he was working.

The sun began to peep in at a corner of the window overlooking the street, and, when he heard the sound of a rider passing by the office, McCabe went to the window and peered out, but thick dust clinging to the panes obstructed his view and he saw no more than a hazy figure jogging into town. He drew his gun and checked the weapon, then pulled Conn's gun from his waistband and examined it. He returned the pistol to his waistband and sat down again at the desk.

Several times in the next thirty minutes he heard footsteps passing the office door and tensed for action. But the door was not opened and he sat chafing mentally at the inaction. Then light footsteps sounded on the sidewalk and the door was opened. A young woman dressed like a waitress entered and paused on the threshold, looking expectantly towards the desk. She carried a notebook in her hand.

McCabe got to his feet, the thumb of his right hand resting on the cartridges in the loops on his gun-belt. 'Ain't you out and about a mite early, Miss?' he demanded. 'What can I do for you?'

'Your breakfast order please,' she replied.

'Breakfast order?' McCabe shook his head. He was hungry, but could not believe that she was interested in what he would like to eat.

'Where's the sheriff;' She looked around questioningly. 'I work in the café along the street. We supply this office with food. How many prisoners have you got locked up?'

'Three so far.'

'So you'll want three breakfasts. What about you? Do you want something to eat?'

'I could eat a horse,' McCabe replied.'

She smiled. 'I'm afraid horsemeat is not on the menu today. Would you like a standard breakfast?'

'Sure thing, and plenty of coffee.' McCabe watched her turn to depart and opened his mouth to recall her, mindful of Frank Holbrooke's order to arrest everyone who came into the office. But she had not come to see the sheriff specifically and he let her go.

Twenty minutes later the street door was thrust open and a youth entered the office carrying a large, covered tray. He left the street door wide open and came towards the desk, staggering a little under the weight. McCabe quickly cleared a corner of the desk so that the tray could be set down.

'Four breakfasts,' the youngster announced, holding out a sheet of paper. 'Sign for them.'

McCabe took the paper, scanned it, then picked up a pen to sign it. At that moment his back was to the open door, his attention diverted, and when a board just inside the door creaked warningly he turned swiftly, dropping the pen and reaching for the butt of his gun. Two men were crowding into the office, guns held ready in their hands, and McCabe stayed his movement and raised his hands, his expression bleak. One of the men was Dave Thorn, and the gambler was grinning.

'You got sense,' Thorn said, 'although

it won't do you no good. When Blade Conn didn't come back to me I guessed something was wrong so I got Ruth to check out the office when she came for the breakfast order. She described you dead to rights, McCabe, so here I am. Where's Conn? I sent him to check with Sarran. What have you done with him?'

'He's still checking with Sarran.' McCabe lifted his hands shoulder high. 'In the cells, where they both belong.'

The youth turned to depart and closed the street door at his back. McCabe watched Thorn carefully as the gambler came towards him, grinning triumphantly.

'You ain't so tough, McCabe. What's the idea locking Sarran in his own jail? You didn't think you could get away with that, did you? Keep him covered, Bill, and shoot him if he looks like trying anything.'

Thorn moved around McCabe at arm's length and snaked the gun out of McCabe's holster. Then he picked up the cell keys and moved to the back of the office.

'Keep watching him, Bill, while I turn the prisoners loose,' Thorn ordered.

The man by the street door grinned and waggled the gun in his hand. 'Just let him try something,' he said.

McCabe was mindful of the gun in his waistband nestling against his spine, which was concealed by his jacket. He half turned to watch Thorn enter the cell block and to cover his left side. Dropping his arms, he clasped his hands behind him, and was relieved when the gunman made no objection. The fingers of his right hand closed around the butt of Conn's gun, and at that moment the street door was thrust open and a man entered.

McCabe pulled the gun from his waistband and exploded into action. He shook the office with a shot that hit the gunman covering him high in the chest. The man twisted and thudded to the floor, his trigger finger jerking spasmodically to send a bullet ploughing into the dusty boards at McCabe's feet. The man who had entered the office halted abruptly and reached for his holstered gun. McCabe fired again, aiming for a shoulder, and the man fell back against the doorpost. His heels caught against the step and he crashed over backwards to fall heavily upon the sidewalk.

McCabe moved quickly across the office to the opposite corner, thumbing back the hammer of his gun as he did so. Dave Thorn appeared in the inner doorway, gun ready, and McCabe shot him in the gun arm just above the elbow. The office shook at the detonations, and gunsmoke plumed across it. Thorn dropped his gun, and clutched at his wounded arm. McCabe crossed to him, swinging his gun, and slammed the barrel against Thorn's head. The gambler went down like a stricken buffalo.

McCabe was breathing heavily. He glanced into the cell block, saw that

Thorn had not been able to unlock any of the cells, and turned his attention to the man writhing in agony on the floor. Kicking a pistol out of the man's reach, he stepped outside to check the man on the sidewalk, who was unconscious. McCabe grasped a handful of the man's shirt and dragged him into the office. As he straightened a townsman came running up and peered in through the doorway.

McCabe looked at the townsman, decided that he posed no threat, and grasped him by an arm.

'You know where the doctor lives?' he demanded. The man nodded. 'Then go fetch him. Send him here and make it fast.'

The man departed at a run and McCabe drew a deep breath. He checked both wounded men for weapons, and picked up the discarded guns and placed them on the desk. Taking a small hideout gun, a .41 derringer, from a holster under Thorn's left armpit, he thrust it into a pocket on his leather vest and then picked up the cell keys from where Thorn had dropped them. He had expected to be wasting his time here in the office, but things were moving.

Unlocking a cell, McCabe dragged the three wounded men inside and locked the door. Sarran was standing at the bars of his cell, gripping them tightly, his knuckles white. He met McCabe's harsh gaze but did not speak, and McCabe grinned and shook his gun in the sheriff's face before going back to the office and crossing to the street door.

When he looked along the street, McCabe saw the townsman returning with Doc Miller, who was carrying a black medical bag. Other men were converging on the office, and McCabe watched them with narrowed gaze. He wondered what effect the shooting would have on Holbrooke's plan to trap Gotch and his bunch.

When the doctor entered the office, McCabe slammed the door on the approaching townsmen and shot home the bolt.

'This way, Doc,' he said, rattling the cell keys, and led the way into the cell block. Thorn was sitting up in the cell, groaning and rubbing his head. Blood showed on his right sleeve, and he got unsteadily to his feet as McCabe unlocked the cell door.

'You'll pay for this, McCabe,' he rasped.

McCabe entered the cell and thrust a hand against Thorn's chest, pushing him backwards. Thorn fell upon the bunk and sat cursing. The doctor entered the cell to examine the other wounded men. McCabe looked around. Blade Conn was now sitting up in his cell, holding his head in his hands. He gazed at McCabe with all the fury of an enraged buffalo in his eyes.

'McCabe,' Sarran called urgently.

McCabe turned to look at the sheriff and froze instantly, for the crooked lawman was holding a sixgun in his right hand and the muzzle was thrust forward between the bars, gaping at McCabe's chest. 'Drop your gun and kick it aside,' Sarran rasped, his dark eyes gleaming. 'Do it quick or you're dead, mister.'

McCabe looked into the black muzzle of the unwavering gun. His instinct was to resist, but there was no mistaking the stark threat in the sheriff's manner and he opened his fingers and let the gun thud to the floor.

'Unlock the cell door,' Sarran continued. 'I want out of here.'

McCabe stepped close to the door of the cell and thrust the key in the lock. 'Where'd you get the gun from?' he demanded.

Sarran laughed gratingly. 'I got friends in this town, mighty powerful friends. It came in through there.' He motioned to the barred window in the back wall of the cell that overlooked the rear of the cell block.

Unlocking the cell door, McCabe stepped back, raising his hands as Sarran emerged from the cell. At that moment a heavy object crashed against the back of McCabe's head and blackness exploded in his mind. He was dimly aware of falling before losing consciousness . . .

Coming back to his senses, McCabe was aware of sharp, stabbing pains in his head. His forehead was filled with throbbing pain, as if his skull had been kicked by a horse. He opened his eyes and his sight returned. He was lying on the floor of a locked cell, and when he lifted his head to look around he saw Dave Thorn standing outside the cell, a leering grin on his face. The gambler's right arm was bandaged and blood was seeping through the white fabric.

McCabe pushed himself to his feet and sat on the bunk at his side. He put his hands to his face and closed his eyes. His head throbbed painfully with each beat of his pulse.

'You're gonna get more than a headache,' Thorn promised in a gloating tone. 'You made a big mistake when you came sticking your long nose into our business.'

McCabe lifted his head and looked around. The doctor had gone, and the two wounded men were lying on bunks in a cell. At that moment Sarran came into the cell block, followed by Blade Conn, who was carrying a shotgun in his big hands.

'You can get him outa here now,' the sheriff said, unlocking the cell door. 'On your feet, McCabe. You're finished around here. Take him outa the rear door and along the back lots. Don't let anyone see you. Thorn, you and Conn better not lose him.'

'He won't get away from me,' Conn said thickly, grinning at McCabe. 'I'm itching to give him his come-uppance. Just let him try something.'

McCabe left the cell and Conn thrust the twin muzzles of the shotgun between McCabe's shoulder-blades. Thorn opened the rear door of the cell block and stepped aside for McCabe to precede him. McCabe blinked in the growing sunlight as he started across the back lots with the two hardcases behind him. He heard the back door of the jail slam, and a heavy bolt was rammed home.

'Where are you taking me?' McCabe demanded.

'You'll be leaving town with Sam Gotch when he's ready to ride,' Thorn said. 'You been wanting to meet Gotch ever since you hit the county, ain't you?'

McCabe did not reply. He looked around. They were following the rear of the buildings fronting the street, and, when they reached the rear of the saloon, Thorn went ahead and opened the back door of the building. McCabe glanced around as Conn ushered him inside. He saw that the early morning sky was burnished by the rising sun.

Jed Grant came along the passage that led into the front of the saloon. He looked as if he had not slept during the night. His hair was tousled and he was wearing a dark silk dressing-gown.

'I don't want him in here,' he said pugnaciously. 'What are you trying to do, Thorn, ruin me?'

'It won't be for long. Gotch will take him out've town when he leaves after the bank job.'

'You're getting me in too deep for my liking,' the saloonman retorted. 'I wish I'd never fallen for your deal.'

'You'll do all right when the loose ends are tied up,' Thorn retorted. 'Blade, let's put him upstairs in the room with the girl. They'll go out've town together when the time comes. Gotch can have the trouble of getting rid of them. It's partly his fault that we've got these problems.'

McCabe ascended the back stairs. His head had cleared somewhat, but he was afforded no chance of getting the better of his captors. Conn was too careful to take any chances, and the twin muzzles of the fear-some weapon he was carrying were warning enough for McCabe to obey without hesitation.

Thorn unbarred a door on the top floor and McCabe was thrust inside. The door was slammed and bolted as he staggered across the room, which was empty except for a single bed and a couple of chairs. A woman's figure was stretched out on the bed, and a pang stabbed through McCabe when he recognized Rosie Dean, who was bound and gagged, her eyes staring in fright above the kerchief over her mouth.

McCabe looked around. There seemed little chance of escape. A window overlooked the rear of the saloon but it was barred, and there was no movement in the bars when he grasped and shook them with all his strength. He turned his attention to the girl and dropped to one knee to untie her. When he removed the gag she spoke shrilly, and McCabe gazed at her for a moment, disconcerted by the invective she screamed at him.

'Why did you kill Billy?' she demanded at length.

'Who said I did?' he countered, straightening to sit on the edge of the bed, his head in his hands.

'Blade Conn. You found out Billy was passing Wells Fargo information to Gotch and his gang.'

'Billy was already dead when I learned that.' McCabe shook his head. 'As far as I know, Conn killed your brother. What happened when you were on your way to meet me? Harpley said you went into the Wells Fargo office like a tornado and dragged Billy away. What spooked you? I saw you on the street minutes earlier going towards the law office and you didn't seem hazed.'

'I was told you were laying a trap for Billy. I had to get him out of town so I got him away from Harpley and sent him to saddle a couple of horses. I went home to get what money I had and Al Spooner was waiting at my cabin for me. I told him I was on the dodge from you and he brought me here. I've been tied up ever since.'

'So Al Spooner was in on the crooked business, huh? That's why he was waiting for me outside your cabin. He must have figured I'd come looking for you when you didn't show up at the law office. And later, Blade Conn told you I had killed Billy, huh?'

The girl nodded. Her eyes were bright with unshed tears. McCabe felt sorry for her.

'I heard that Billy was feeding information to the outlaws on the say-so of Frank Holbrooke, the chief detective for Wells Fargo,' he said softly. 'A trap for the gang was being set, and Billy was in on it, on the right side. You can be proud of your brother, Rosie.'

'But he's dead,' she said bitterly. 'His young life is wasted. Nobody had any right to get him mixed up with those outlaws.'

'Nobody figured he would get hurt.' McCabe arose and went around the room looking for weak spots. He checked the door and could not budge it. Returning to the window, he tried the bars again but they resisted his efforts. 'Does anyone come up here and check on you?' he demanded.

'I was brought food last night, but I haven't seen anyone since. What are they going to do, McCabe? Are they going to kill me?'

'Not if I can stop them.' McCabe felt in his vest pockets and produced the .41 calibre derringer he had taken from Dave Thorn. He checked the weapon and found both barrels loaded. Looking at Rosie through narrowed eyes, he drew a deep breath. 'If you wanta get outa here you should maybe make some noise,' he suggested.

She stared at him for several moments, then nodded slowly and walked to the door and banged on it. McCabe sat on the foot of the bed, the derringer concealed in his right hand. Minutes passed and there was no reply to the noise Rosie was making. She tired of hammering with her fists and turned her back to the door and started kicking at it with her heel.

The door suddenly shook under a loud crash as someone outside hammered upon it with a heavy fist. Rosie backed away in shock, looking at McCabe.

'Stop that racket in there,' Blade Conn shouted through the panels.

'Open the door,' Rosie replied in a shrill tone. 'Let me out of here.' She hammered on the door again.

McCabe heard the door being unbolted. Rosie moved back into the centre of the room as Conn thrust the door open with such violence it crashed against the wall. Conn was holding a gun in his right hand and it swung instantly to cover McCabe, who did not move.

'What's all the noise about?' Conn demanded. 'I told you to shut up.'

He stepped towards Rosie, lifting his left hand as if to strike her, and for a moment his attention was not on McCabe. Rosie instantly stepped to her left, moving between Conn and McCabe, and she wrapped her arms around Conn's gunarm.

McCabe left the foot of the bed like an uncoiling spring. Conn was trying to shake loose of Rosie, and McCabe grabbed the man's gun wrist, at the same time thrusting the muzzle of the derringer between the big man's eyes. Rosie was trapped between them, pinioned by their straining bodies.

'Let go of your gun,' McCabe snapped. 'Let me have it or you're dead, Conn.'

Conn glared at McCabe with defiance in his eyes, but he could not ignore the gunmuzzle pressing against his forehead and he opened his fingers, permitting McCabe to grasp his sixgun. McCabe stepped backwards and Rosie scuttled out of the line of fire. McCabe thrust the derringer back into his pocket and took Conn's pistol into his right hand. He stepped forward and smashed his left fist against Conn's jaw. The big man tried to avoid the blow but was too slow and fell to his hands and knees.

McCabe struck Conn across the back of the head with the barrel of the pistol and Conn flattened out on the floor.

'Get the rope you were tied with,' McCabe rapped, and Rosie hurried to the bed. She held out the rope and McCabe used it to bind Conn's wrists behind his back. He straightened. 'Now let's get out of here,' he said. 'Stick close to me, Rosie.'

Gun in hand, McCabe left the room, closing the door and bolting it. He checked the stairs. The saloon was quiet at this time in the morning and he glanced at Rosie.

'We're gonna get outa here,' he rasped. 'You can stay with me, Rosie, or take off and hide yourself somewhere until this is settled. I think you'll be safer with me but I've got things to do and time is wasting.'

'I'll stick with you,' she replied, 'and I'll back you if I can.'

'You're doing all right,' McCabe encouraged. 'Let's go.'

He led the way down the stairs, gun ready for action, and at that moment shots rang out from the direction of the main street. McCabe was startled, but the noise was enough to set him into action. He hurled himself down the rest of the stairs and ran to the back door with Rosie hurrying to keep up with him.

9

McCabe left the saloon and hastened across the back lots towards the jail, determined to get back on track and follow Frank Holbrooke's instructions. He was supposed to be holding the jail with the sheriff locked in a cell. There was still time to do that, and as he ran he looked around. The back lots were deserted, and he reached the alley beside the jail and paused for breath. Rosie arrived beside him as he hastened along the alley to the main street.

Peering around, he saw gunsmoke drifting both sides of the street in front of the saloon, and frowned as he tried to understand what was happening. Gotch and his bunch were not supposed to hit the bank this early, so what was the shooting about?

He glanced to his right and saw Sarran standing in the doorway of the law office, looking along the street. But the lawman had no interest in the shooting and retreated into the office and closed the door. McCabe left his cover and went forward grimly, drawing Conn's sixgun. The weapon was cocked and ready as he thrust open the door of the office and lunged inside, his teeth clenched and his nerves on edge.

His action took the sheriff by surprise. Sarran was bending over his desk, his back to the street door, and he whirled around as McCabe crashed into the office. The sheriff instinctively lifted his right hand to his holstered gun.

'Don't do it,' McCabe warned, and the sheriff reluctantly raised his hands shoulder high. McCabe closed with him, jerking the sheriff's gun out of its holster. 'Now let's get back to where we were an hour ago,' he said harshly. 'You know the way to the cells.'

Sarran shook his head and took up the bunch of keys on his desk. He unlocked the connecting door and led the way into the cell block. When he walked into the cell with the barred window overlooking the rear of the building McCabe laughed and grasped the sheriff's shoulder.

'Try another one this time,' he suggested. 'That one at the end on the left looks like it will do. I don't want you to get your hands on another gun, huh?'

Sarran shrugged and handed over the cell keys. He entered the cell McCabe had indicated and sat down on the foot of the bunk. McCabe locked the door and returned to the office.

The street door was open and McCabe saw a big man, dressed in dirty range clothes, standing on the threshold talking to Rosie, who had seated herself behind the sheriff's desk. The man was wearing twin sixguns on cartridge belts crossed around his waist.

'Who are you?' McCabe demanded. His gun was still in his hand and pointing at the newcomer.

'Jabez Eke,' the man replied. 'I got

orders from Frank Holbrooke to come in here and take over from you.'

'Is this Jabez Eke?' McCabe asked Rosie and she nodded.

'Right.' McCabe smiled. 'I have to be careful. Glad to know you, Eke.'

Eke came into the office with out-stretched hand, and McCabe holstered his gun and shook hands with him.

'You know what to do?' McCabe asked.

'Sure. I'm to hold this place until Holbrooke arrives, and I arrest and jail everyone who shows up in between.'

'Good.' McCabe went to the door. 'See you later.'

Eke nodded and sat down on a corner of the desk, facing the street door. Rosie slid off the chair behind the desk and almost ran towards McCabe.

'I'm coming with you,' she said.

'Mebbe I could do with your help at that.' McCabe nodded. 'I'm on my way to pick up Art Pell and I don't know what he looks like. You can point him out to me.'

'Pell? Have you got anything on that crooked lawyer?'

McCabe shook his head. 'I don't know a thing about him, but I've been told to get him so I'll bring him in.'

He left the office with Rosie following and moved into the alley beside the jail. Rosie stared questioningly at him.

'I need to stay clear of the street,' he explained. 'Dave Thorn is out there somewhere, and if he sees me loose it could ruin a few plans. I need to get Pell into jail fast, and meeting up with Thorn right now could sidetrack me again. Now I'm back on schedule I want to stay that way. Can you get to the lawyer's house by the back ways?'

'Just follow me.' Rosie spoke fiercely. 'I can't wait to see Art Pell behind bars.'

The girl led the way to the back lots, McCabe following closely. The shooting along the street had ended and an uneasy silence seemed to have settled over the town.

Rosie reached the rear of the row of

houses on the west side of North Street and hurried along almost to where they adjoined West Street. She paused in the shelter of a barn at the rear of a large house and looked up into McCabe's brooding face.

'Pell lives here,' she said curtly. 'Can I see you arrest him?'

'I want you to point him out to me,' McCabe replied. 'Come on. I need to get back to the jail fast. I don't have any time to lose.'

Rosie followed him to the rear of the house and McCabe rapped on the back door, which was opened almost immediately by a small man in a dressing-gown. Beady brown eyes regarded McCabe suspiciously.

'Art Pell?' McCabe demanded.

'He's Pell,' Rosie said from behind McCabe.

The lawyer's eyes narrowed and he opened his mouth.

'Save it,' McCabe interrupted. 'I've got orders to throw you in the jug, Pell, so come along without trouble.'

'You've got no right to arrest me,' Pell spluttered.

McCabe palmed his gun and the three clicks as he cocked the powerful weapon sounded sharply metallic in the early morning.

'This gives me all the rights I need,' he said. 'We can do this however you want, but I advise you not to give me any trouble. Come on, Pell.'

'Where's the sheriff?' Pell demanded. 'I want to talk to him.'

'Sure.' McCabe laughed. 'He'll be in the next cell to yours. You can jaw his head off if you want.'

'I need to get dressed first,' Pell protested.

'No time now. Do you have a wife?'

'I do.'

'Then tell her to bring some clothes along to the law office, but not before ten.' McCabe was aware of a woman in the room behind the lawyer, and at his words she came forward, pushing her husband aside.

'If you're arresting Art on the say-so

214

of Rosie Dean then you're making a big mistake,' she told McCabe.

'I ain't doin' that, ma'am,' he replied. 'Rosie ain't got a thing to do with it. She's along just to make sure it's Art I get.'

He grasped the lawyer's shoulder and almost lifted him over the doorstep. Pell struggled ineffectually, but McCabe took him by the collar and returned along the back lots. Rosie followed, taunting Pell. When they reached the law office, McCabe found the place quiet, and Eke reported no disturbance.

Pell was lodged in a cell next to the sheriff, and fell to bending Sarran's ear about being arrested.

'What do you think I can do about it?' Sarran demanded. 'I need someone to get me out've here.'

'And that ain't gonna happen.' McCabe left the cell block and locked the door, then dropped the keys on the desk. He looked speculatively at Rosie, who was sitting on the seat behind the desk. 'I figure it would be safe enough for you to go to the eating house and bring us some breakfast back, huh?' he demanded. 'I'm hung over with the need to fill the empty space beneath my ribs.'

'I don't figure it is safe,' Rosie replied. 'Dan Bocker supplies food to the jail, and he never charges Dave Thorn for meals, so I figure he and Thorn are mighty friendly, or else Thorn has something on Bocker. But if you're that hungry I could go to the café where I work and get you something.'

McCabe shook his head. 'On second thoughts it could be too dangerous to let you out of my sight after what's happened,' he mused. 'I guess I can see this through without breakfast.'

'There's nothing to stop you going yourself,' Eke said. 'I'm here to watch things.'

'Yeah. But my orders are to bring in Pell and then stay here to side you.' McCabe shook his head. 'Frank

Holbrooke made that plenty clear and I ain't about to disobey him. He crossed to a chair standing behind the door and sat down to relax.

Boots thudding on the sidewalk outside the office minutes later alerted McCabe and he stood up, his hand on the butt of his gun. The door was thrust open and two men entered in a hurry. McCabe moved backwards a couple of quick paces to avoid being hit by the opening door. He recognized the foremost as Rattlesnake Riley, and the outlaw was not expecting trouble because his gun was still in its holster. McCabe instantly set his right hand into motion, drawing his big gun and cocking it in a split second. He levelled it at the tall outlaw.

Riley halted quickly and the man at his back collided with him. They fell apart, and Riley made a play for his holstered gun. McCabe stepped in and crashed his gun barrel against Riley's right elbow, numbing the man's gun arm. Riley's weapon thudded to the floor and McCabe slid to the left, getting out of arm's length and covering the second man, who was in the act of drawing his gun.

'Don't finish that draw, mister,' Eke rapped, and McCabe threw a glance in his direction to see Eke standing with both guns drawn and levelled at the newcomers. 'This is Rattlesnake Riley,' Eke continued, 'and the other one is Rafe Carter, who rides for Joel Slater.'

'I know them both by sight,' McCabe acknowledged, closing on Carter and jerking the man's gun from its holster. 'Carter left the JS last evening in the company of Sam Gotch himself. I threw Riley in jail along with Dave Thorn but someone turned them loose. Welcome back, Riley. This just isn't one of your days, huh? You came to see Sarran, I guess. Well you've got all the time in the world to talk to him.'

Riley stood motionless, grasping his right elbow with the fingers of his left hand. His eyes were narrowed, and had the look of a wild animal in their depths. But McCabe had no intention of taking any chances with his kind.

'Search 'em both carefully, Eke, and then we'll put them behind bars. I'm beginning to see why Holbrooke wanted two of us in here. It looks like the whole gang will wander in before this business is done.'

Eke holstered his guns and searched the two hard-cases. He removed a knife from Riley and another gun from Carter. McCabe stood by with his gun ready, and Eke picked up the cell keys and led the way into the rear of the jail.

'What's going on here!?' Riley demanded when he saw Sarran in a cell.

'It's round-up time on your kind,' McCabe told him. 'What did you want with Sarran?'

'Go ask Gotch,' Riley snarled.

'You think I won't get around to that?' McCabe grinned. 'Lock 'em in the cell next to Sarran's, Eke, so they can talk without shouting. Not that it will do 'em any good.'

Eke locked the two men in a cell and McCabe walked to the back door and checked it. The door was merely bolted although there was a big key in its lock. McCabe locked the door, removed the key and dropped it into his pocket before following Eke back into the front office.

Rosie was standing by the window overlooking the street, peering out through the dusty pane. Her face was taut with fear when she glanced at McCabe.

'A bunch of riders have just ridden into town,' she warned. 'About fifteen of them, headed by Joel Slater.'

McCabe hurried to the window and peered out at the street. He saw the riders cantering in a tight bunch towards the saloon, and wondered where Frank Holbrooke was at that moment and what he was doing.

'Do you figure Slater is gonna take a hand in this?' Eke demanded.

'I don't know a damn thing!' McCabe shook his head. 'Frank is playing this one close to his vest. All we can do is take it as she comes.' He moved away from the window and drew his sixgun, glancing at Rosie as he did so. 'You'd better make yourself scarce, Rosie,' he said. 'There must be places around town that will be less dangerous for you than this one. Why don't you head out and take cover somewhere until this is over?'

'I'd rather stay here,' she replied firmly. 'You've got Art Pell behind bars and I want to see him get his deserts.'

Eke had taken McCabe's place at the window and was watching the street.

'See anything interesting?' McCabe called.

'Slater is going into the saloon with most of his riders. But three of them are riding back this way. Could be they're coming to see what's happened to Sarran. I got a feeling the sheriff should be out there in the thick of things to show his support, and they're missing him.'

'If they keep coming in twos and threes then we can handle this deal,' McCabe said with a grin. 'We got plenty of room in the cells.'

He went to Eke's side and peered through the window. Three riders were coming at a trot back along the street, and they swung in towards the hitch-rail outside the law office. McCabe watched them dismount, and when they moved towards the door he crossed the office to stand in a corner facing it, his gun in his hand. Eke positioned himself opposite, taking up a crossfire position.

The door was thrust open and the foremost of the trio, a tall, heavily built man wearing twin sixguns, came into the office, his spurs jingling musically.

'Hey, Sarran, why the hell ain't you in the saloon?' he called. 'Jed Grant says it's time you showed up.'

He fell silent when he failed to see the sheriff in the office, and stared at Rosie, who was sitting, pale-faced and tense, in the chair behind the desk.

'What's goin' on here?' he demanded. 'Where the hell is Sarran?'

McCabe cocked his gun. 'I'll take you to Sarran,' he said. 'Just keep your hands away from your guns. Call your pards in. I want them to join us. Do it now and don't make the mistake of trying to beat this deal.'

The other two men were waiting on the sidewalk, still interested in what was happening outside the saloon.

'Do like the man says, Drogo,' Eke rapped from his side of the office, and the newcomer turned his head and looked into the muzzles of Eke's drawn guns. 'This guy is Drogo Taylor, McCabe,' Eke continued. 'He's Joel Slater's top gun. Holbrooke has said that Taylor was involved in at least one of the stagecoach raids.'

'He'd better start doing what I told him or he'll suddenly lose all interest in this business,' McCabe rasped. 'What about it, Taylor?'

The gunman narrowed his eyes as if

calculating the odds against him. Then he grinned and relaxed, lifting his hands shoulder high. 'I never play against a stacked deck,' he said, shaking his head, 'and it looks to me like someone is calling these shots. Deal me out.'

'Call your pards inside,' McCabe rapped.

'No siree! You want 'em, you call 'em in. I'm outa this.' Drogo Taylor shook his head emphatically.

One of the two men on the sidewalk turned towards the door and peered into the office. When he saw Taylor with his hands raised he made a play for his gun, leaping for the cover of the door jamb on the right as he did so. His yell of warning alerted his companion and the man vanished to the left of the door before McCabe could fire.

Eke moved forward quickly and jammed the muzzle of one of his guns against Taylor's breastbone. He disarmed the gunman quickly and forced him to lie face down on the dusty boards. A hand holding a gun appeared around the door jamb and began bracketing the office with slugs. The shots blasted raucously, and McCabe ducked as the first bullet breathed in his left ear. He returned fire instantly, sending two shots through the front wall of the office, his breathing restrained because of the gunsmoke swirling about his head.

The gunman outside stepped jerkily into the doorway, his gun spilling from his suddenly nerveless fingers. He twisted slowly and pitched on to his face to lie motionless on the boardwalk.

McCabe stepped into the doorway. A bullet splintered the door jamb beside his head and he crouched and went out to the sidewalk, his gun lining up on the remaining gunman, who was attempting to spring into his saddle. McCabe triggered a shot that hit the man in the side of the neck, and then held his fire as the gunman yelled thinly in shock before pitching over backwards to lie unmoving in the dust.

The shots reverberated across the town, and McCabe could hear several dogs barking at the disturbance. He blinked against the gunsmoke and looked towards the saloon one hundred yards along the street. Men were already emerging from the building to stand and look enquiringly towards the law office.

Stepping back inside the office, McCabe closed the door and bolted it. Rosie was still sitting behind the desk, and looked to be frozen there. Eke was ushering Drogo Taylor into the cell block. McCabe heard the prisoners demanding to know what the shooting was about but Eke did not speak, and reappeared after locking his prisoner in a cell.

'So far so good,' Eke remarked.

'It looks like it could hot up very shortly,' McCabe replied, peering through the window. 'Yeah. There are half a dozen riders coming this way now.'

'We can hold 'em off.' Eke spoke

confidently. 'I guess this is why Holbrooke wanted the two of us in here, huh?'

'You could be right.' McCabe reloaded his gun and took up one of the sixguns Eke had removed from Taylor. He checked the weapon and stuck it into his waistband, then looked out the window yet again. 'Here they come,' he announced.

'Hey, you in the office,' a harsh voice called. 'Send the sheriff out. He's wanted.'

'He's wanted all right,' McCabe replied loudly, and Eke laughed.

'You got ten seconds to send Sarran out here,' the voice continued, and McCabe risked a look through the big window. He saw the six men sitting their mounts in a semicircle in the centre of the street, facing the office, and noted that they were holding their sixguns. He moved away from the window, and had barely reached his corner when a fusillade of shots rang out and the front window shattered.

Glass flew across the office, and Eke ducked away to protect his face. McCabe drew his gun and crouched, covering the window.

Two of the riders spurred their horses to the left, and McCabe heard them going along the alley beside the office, making for the rear of the jail.

'Open that inner door and keep an eye on the rear,' McCabe said sharply, and Eke obeyed.

The four riders remaining outside began to empty their guns into the office, and slugs crackled and slammed around. McCabe crouched and eased forward until he could peer out at a lower corner of the window. Lifting his gun, he triggered the weapon fast, hurling a string of lead at the riders, his eyes slitted and teeth bared in a silent snarl of defiance.

Two of the riders pitched out of leather immediately and the remaining two hauled their mounts around and retreated quickly. McCabe aimed at one of them and fired, grunting his satisfaction when the rider cartwheeled out of his saddle and thudded into the dust.

Eke fired two shots into the cell block, and as the noise faded he glanced at McCabe, a grin on his taut face. 'Someone took a look through the window back there,' he reported. 'I figure I've discouraged him some.'

'They need reinforcements out front,' McCabe replied. He looked at Rosie, who was crouching on the floor behind the desk. 'You all right?' he demanded, reloading his gun, and the girl nodded. Her eyes were wide with fear, her hands clenched.

'I'd rather be here than anywhere,' she replied.

McCabe went back to the window and peered out. An uneasy silence existed outside, and he looked at the three motionless bodies lying in the dust of the wide street. A figure moved just outside to the left, and a man thrust a gun into the office at the far left corner. McCabe lifted his sixgun, fired two swift shots, and the man uttered a yell of pain and whirled away.

'One of the two who went along the alley,' McCabe called to Eke. 'They're determined to get in here, huh?'

Silence resettled, and McCabe wrinkled his nose against the acrid bite of gunsmoke. He wondered what was happening in other parts of the town, and his curiosity increased when a spate of shots blasted out the silence at the far end of the street. He went to the door and opened it, edging cautiously into the doorway, and a bullet smacked into the jamb at his side. He saw gunsmoke pluming out of an alley opposite and aimed at it, his deadly gun blasting quickly.

The shooting along the street rolled on like thunder, and McCabe stepped outside and planted his back against the front wall of the office, covering his immediate area. Nothing happened, and he figured that the remaining rider had departed to make a report on the situation at the jail. He looked along the street and saw gunsmoke drifting thickly around the saloon. There were men opposite the saloon who were firing into the building, and a spirited resistance from Jed Grant's place added to the noise and apparent confusion. Echoes were rolling and thundering, and dogs were barking frantically in the background.

McCabe itched to take a hand in the fight but would not disobey Holbrooke's orders. He went back into the office and closed the door, although his inclination was to take the fight to the badmen. But as he was unaware of Holbrooke's strategy he dared not take action for fear of doing the wrong thing.

The shooting along the street faded away and an uneasy silence settled. McCabe reloaded his deadly gun and remained in his corner, covering the door and the big front window. He moistened his lips and told himself that it looked like being a long day. Tense moments passed and nothing happened. The growling echoes of the shooting no longer muttered in the distance. Peace seemed to have resettled over the town, but McCabe was not fooled by this respite. In his estimation there was still a long way to go.

'Hey, inside the office!'

McCabe tensed as the voice came from just outside. He cocked his gun and waited.

'Frank Holbrooke sent me with a message for Cole McCabe.'

'I'm McCabe. What's on your mind?'

'Holbrooke said for you to get to the rear of the saloon and go in. All the badmen are forted up inside, and he wants you to chase 'em out.'

'On my own?' McCabe demanded.

'Holbrooke says it's a one-man chore and you're elected. He figgers you're the best man he's got.'

McCabe grimaced at the words. 'Thanks for nothing,' he replied. 'Tell Holbrooke I'm on my way.'

'You can't go into the saloon on your own,' Eke protested as McCabe took a second sixgun off the desk and checked that it was ready for action.

'Getting in there will be the easy part,' McCabe opined, thrusting the second gun into his waistband. 'I'm more concerned about what will happen after I'm in there. If you figger you'll be able to handle this end of the deal then let me out the back door and I'll get to work. I was beginning to think Holbrooke had left me out of the big round-up.'

He grinned at Rosie, who shook her head silently and made no effort to follow him. Preceding Eke into the cell block, he unlocked the back door and cautiously peered outside. The back lots were apparently deserted and he took his leave of Eke and walked resolutely towards the rear of the saloon, gun in hand and nerves hair-triggered.

This was more like it, he thought, checking his surroundings at each step, and this was where he started to prove his reputation.

10

McCabe stayed close to the rear of the buildings fronting the main street and moved fast towards the saloon, watching his surroundings intently for he expected the badmen to be covering their backs. Pausing in the shelter of a barn at the rear of the saloon, he studied the tall building, and was startled when a voice spoke to him from inside the barn. He flattened himself against the rough boards.

'McCabe, we're covering you,' the voice said.

'Harpley!' McCabe was surprised. 'Who's inside the saloon?'

'Joel Slater and the rest of his bunch with Jed Grant and his gunnies. There's about a dozen of them, and Frank figures you can stir 'em into making a break for it.'

'I'll do my best,' McCabe muttered.

'I guess I'll have to play it as she comes. What's the word on Gotch and his bunch?'

'They ain't been seen. Everything went wrong this morning. Holbrooke wants the town cleaned out, then you can go after Gotch.'

McCabe smiled grimly. 'That's what I figure. I'd best get moving then. See you around, Harpley.'

'Watch your step,' came the harsh reply.

McCabe studied the rear of the saloon. The back wall contained a door, one ground-floor window and two windows on the first floor. To the left of the ground-floor window there was a one-storey building abutting the main structure which was without a door or windows. McCabe figured it was a storeroom with interior access. He saw no movement anywhere around the back of the place and set out across the fifty yards between the barn and the saloon. His gun was clenched in his right hand and he was ready to slip into action at the first sign of trouble.

He was disappointed that Gotch and his gang had not been seen, but dismissed them from his mind. If he managed to get among the hardcases in the saloon there was a very good chance of ending this trouble quickly, and then he could continue with his original task — the obliteration of the Gotch gang.

Shooting suddenly erupted on the street facing the saloon, and McCabe guessed that Holbrooke planned to keep the hardcases busy in order to cover his entry into the rear of the building. He sprinted forward and gained the back wall, flattening himself against the sun-warped boards beside the door. He tried the door, found it locked, and, looking at the ground-floor window, saw thick bars fixed solidly across the glass and dismissed the thought of gaining an entrance by either means.

The storeroom attracted his attention and he went to it, holstering his gun. He found that he could easily grasp the edge of the flat roof, and within seconds he had hauled himself upwards and was lying on the roof. Gasping from his exertions, he was intrigued to see a trap-door in the roof and got to his knees to test it. The trap-door was ill fitting, and he was able to force his fingers under it. Getting to his feet, he took a firm hold on the edge of the trap and exerted his considerable strength. After moments of heaving upwards there was a sharp crack and the trap-door came away in his hands. He staggered backwards and almost fell off the roof, but regained his balance and drew his gun.

Peering down through the trap, he saw boxes and crates of merchandise stacked inside, and quickly entered, swinging to the floor. There was an inner door. He eased it open and peered out into a passage. The silence was intense and he saw no one around. But he was not fooled by the air of desertion. Cocking his gun, he emerged from the store and moved cautiously along the passage.

The back stairs were on the left and he ascended them quickly. Every board creaked under his weight and he figured that anyone in the saloon must hear his movements. But he reached the upper floor without incident and paused at the closed door of the room where he and Rosie Dean had been imprisoned.

The bolt on the door was disengaged and he opened the door swiftly. He had left Blade Conn inside, and was disappointed to find the room empty. Going on, he searched the upper rooms overlooking the rear of the saloon. All were deserted. Turning his attention to the rooms overlooking the main street, he thrust open the nearest door and surprised two men who were watching the street with rifles in their hands. Both men jerked around as the door was opened, and McCabe covered them swiftly, his gun steady in his hand, the black muzzle of the weapon gaping readily at them.

'Put down the guns,' McCabe rapped, 'and do it fast.'

The men obeyed without hesitation, dropping their rifles and raising their hands. McCabe grimaced, not needing prisoners.

'Listen,' he said harshly. 'I'm gonna take you down and send you out the back door. You'll walk towards the barn out there with your hands raised. I'll be covering you all the way, and I don't want a sound out of you. Got that?'

One man nodded and the other shrugged. McCabe motioned with his gun and they left the room ahead of him, descending the stairs side by side, their hands still raised. McCabe followed closely, and they reached the ground floor without trouble. But as the men turned towards the back door a voice called to them from their left, out of McCabe's sight.

'Where are you two going?'

McCabe, on the bottom stair, leaned forward slightly and looked around the corner of the wall to see Jed Grant standing in the doorway leading into the saloon. The saloonman was holding a rifle, and was in the act of levelling it, sensing that something was wrong. McCabe revealed himself, his gun covering Grant. He saw the saloonman's expression change and spoke quickly.

'Drop the gun and come this way, Grant, or you're dead.'

Grant hesitated, his face turning into a mask as he realized that the chips were down. Then he raised the muzzle of the rifle in an attempt to cover McCabe, who thumbed off a shot. The crash of the detonation rocked the saloon, and Grant was hurled back through the doorway in which he was standing by the force of the bullet striking him. The rifle spilled from his hands and he flung his arms wide as he lost his balance. McCabe saw a splotch of blood on the man's shirtfront before Grant hit the floor.

McCabe went forward quickly, his

attention on the saloon. He heard the back door open, and paused to see his two prisoners fleeing. Dismissing them from his mind, he lunged over Grant's motionless figure and shouldered open the door leading into the big public room. Two quick steps took him inside and he saw at least nine men at the bar, all frozen by the sound of the shot and looking towards him. At his appearance, the men broke out of their paralysis of shock and reached for their guns.

Dropping to one knee, McCabe triggered his pistol, filling the saloon with smoke and gun-thunder. Two men at the bar went down instantly, one after the other, and, as he swung the muzzle of his weapon to encompass the others, hot lead came back at him.

The saloon reverberated under the shock of roaring guns. McCabe flinched when a bullet tugged at his hatbrim. But he kept shooting, triggering his smoking Colt, eyes narrowed against blossoming gunsmoke, his ears protesting painfully at the racket. He felt a flashing pain in his left arm just above the elbow, and reached for the spare gun in his waistband as the hammer of his Colt cracked on a spent chamber.

Dropping flat to avoid the slugs fired at him, he resumed firing with the spare gun, and at that moment the batwings were thrust open and several men came bustling into the saloon from the street, their guns hammering.

McCabe swung his Colt to cover them, then recognized Frank Holbrooke in the lead and pushed himself to his feet. The five hardcases still standing were throwing down their weapons and raising their hands.

Holbrooke advanced upon McCabe, grinning widely. McCabe shook his head and began to reload his weapons. He hated the smell of gunsmoke.

'I knew you'd turn the tide.' Holbrooke was old, in his fifties at least, and his age showed clearly in his face.

'Where's Gotch and his bunch?' McCabe demanded. 'It looks like your plan failed, Frank.'

'That ain't a problem.' Holbrooke shook his head. 'We needed to smoke out the rest of the badmen skulking around town, and we've surely done that. Gotch went to Ash Tolliver's house soon as he hit town and the banker told him a trap had been set and there was no extra money in the bank. Gotch rode out again, but fast, and I figure he headed back to Slater's ranch. That's where he's been lying low for the past couple of months.'

'Then I'd better make tracks.' McCabe reloaded his empty chambers, holstered his gun and stuck the spare weapon into his waistband.

One of the men who had backed Holbrooke came forward to report. 'We got Joel Slater over by the bar, Frank. McCabe nailed him and he ain't got much breath left in him. Do you wanta talk to him before he cashes his chips?'

'I sure do.' Holbrooke crossed the saloon, and McCabe started to follow but changed his mind and walked to the batwings.

The air on the street was clean and sweet and McCabe filled his lungs deeply before exhaling sharply. He was hungry, and the void in his stomach, coupled with gunsmoke fumes, filled him with nausea. He looked around and saw Rosie Dean hurrying towards him along the sidewalk from the law office. Glancing to his left, he saw two men escorting a tall, well-dressed man towards him. At that moment the batwings were thrust open and Holbrooke appeared.

'Ah,' the chief detective declared. 'They're bringing in Tolliver. He's got a lot to answer for. He agreed to help me trap Gotch and his boys, but I guess his own crooked business came first.'

'You know he's crooked?' McCabe studied Tolliver as the man halted in front of them. 'Then it's on the cards that he helped to rob the Deans of their cow spread.'

'Better than that,' Holbrooke retorted. 'He admitted it to me a week ago, and I used the knowledge to lever him into helping me nail Gotch.' He shook his head. 'The dirty double-dealer! He must have thought better of it. Did you throw that crooked lawyer, Art Pell, in jail this morning? I need him behind bars.'

'Just like you told me to.' McCabe nodded. 'Are Thorn and Blade Conn among the men in the saloon?'

'Nope. I saw them leaving town before I could get my men into position. You better get moving, Cole. Gotch is still two jumps ahead of you.'

'Sure. But I ain't leaving until I've put something in my belly,' McCabe responded. He looked at Rosie as the girl came to his side. 'Do you figure we can get some breakfast now?' he asked.

'I'd rather stick around here and keep an eye on Tolliver,' she said. 'He's a snake, and he'll wriggle out've this if he gets half a chance.'

'He won't do that,' Holbrooke assured her. 'And you'll get your pa's ranch back, Rosie.'

The girl sighed heavily and her stiffly held shoulders slumped a little. McCabe saw a world of misery in her pale eyes as she blinked rapidly.

'It's too late for Billy,' she observed bitterly.

McCabe grasped her elbow and tugged her gently. 'Let's get some breakfast,' he urged. 'I still got some action to handle, but I can't even think about it until I've eaten.'

They walked along the street together, and McCabe looked around at the little town. He did not like the way this case had developed, and was aware that Holbrooke's behind-the-scenes activities had spoiled his play. Now he was eager to get away from Holbrooke's influence and finish off the grim business in his own way.

'You won't do anything foolish while I'm gone, Rosie, will you?' he asked.

'Such as?' The girl's tone was sharp.

'Such as riding out to your ranch and trying to take it over.'

'That's just what I'd like to do, but I guess I won't be that stupid. Dave Thorn's got two hardcases out there, Newton and Harmer. They'd gun me down on sight. I guess I'll wait until the range has been cleared of badmen before I venture out there.'

'I'm riding out to JS,' McCabe mused. 'Your spread is on the way, huh?'

'Sure.' She glanced quickly at him. 'You ain't thinking of dropping by there first, are you?'

'Holbrooke said Thorn and Blade Conn split the breeze out of town soon as they realized trouble was on them. I'm thinking Thorn has gone out to your spread.'

'I'll ride with you,' Rosie said instantly.

'Not before I've eaten,' McCabe told her flatly.

They went into the café and McCabe ate a big breakfast, washing it down with two cups of coffee. Rosie merely picked at her food, and sprang up from her seat when McCabe arose.

'I'm ready to hit the trail,' she said excitedly. 'I want to see Thorn and Conn get theirs.'

They went to the stable and saddled their mounts. McCabe was in a hurry to be on his way now, and kept looking around for Holbrooke, afraid the chief detective might appear with a change of orders. But they rode out without incident and headed south at a fast clip. McCabe was silent, thoughtful, steeling himself for the coming showdown. Rosie was tight-lipped, filled with anguish because her brother had not survived the ordeal that had befallen them.

Two hours passed. The sun climbed steadily through the eastern sky, increasing the dry heat until McCabe was sweating freely.

'We better stop here,' Rosie said at length. 'The ranch is just the other side of this ridge. If Thorn is here he'll be watching for someone to follow him from town.'

McCabe slid from his saddle and trailed his reins. He moved to the top of the ridge and dropped flat to squirm up to the skyline. When he saw the ranch headquarters below, small and neat in the stark sunlight, he nodded. This was the kind of place he hoped one day to buy. The thought flashed through the back of his mind as he looked at the corral to check the number of horses present.

'Thorn is here,' Rosie said sharply, and McCabe looked up to see she was standing on the skyline and staring down at the spread. He reached up, grasped her shoulder, and pulled her down to the ground.

'You better stay out of this,' he warned. 'There'll be some lead flying around shortly.'

'That chestnut in the corral is Thorn's favourite horse,' Rosie continued. 'And the bay is Blade Conn's mount. They're both here.'

'You stick around up here where it'll be safe and keep an eye on my back,' McCabe said. 'Can you handle a rifle?'

'Sure. How you gonna handle this? There's at least four of them down there.'

'Just watch me.' McCabe spoke quietly. He took a last look around the spread, absorbing details, then slid back from the skyline. 'You got to stay out of this, Rosie,' he said sternly. 'Don't go getting under my feet.'

'I'll be covering your back,' she replied, and drew his rifle from its scabbard when they reached the horses.

'Don't shoot yourself in the foot,' he warned with a grin, and she scowled.

He swung into his saddle and headed off to the right, riding into a draw that angled down towards the spread and following it to where it petered out on the range to the right of the ranch. Reining in, he picked his route to the rear of the house and rode out of cover to follow it, moving as if he had every right in the world to be there. He had a strange sensation, like an itch, between his shoulder-blades, and suspected that Rosie was following his every movement through the sights of his rifle. He hoped she did not have a nervous trigger finger as he continued on a circuitous approach to the squat buildings, watching intently for movement of any kind.

A small stand of trees masked him from the house on his final approach, and he left his horse tethered to a branch in cover before continuing on foot in the open. He reached the side of the house and moved along it towards the rear corner, and when he reached the corner a cocked pistol was thrust around it to jab him in the stomach. He froze as Blade Conn stepped into view, and lifted his hands away from his waist.

'I saw you coming,' Conn rasped exultantly. 'I got you cold, McCabe. I got you dead to rights. You've come to the end of your rope.'

McCabe fell back a pace and Conn came out from behind the corner, staying close. His fleshy face was filled with grim pleasure.

'I'm gonna be real happy to finish you off, McCabe,' he said gleefully. 'Thorn was wondering how he could get at you.'

'You finished off Billy Dean,' McCabe rasped.

Conn nodded. 'That damn kid was too nosey for his own good. He was playing Sam Gotch for a sucker. Now you turn around and walk along to the porch. Dave'll be real glad to see you, mister.'

McCabe moved out from the side of the house as he turned to obey, and had barely taken a pace forward when a bullet crackled past his right ear so close he fancied he felt the wind of it. Conn cried out in shock and McCabe whirled instantly, reaching for his gun. But Conn was crumpling to the ground, his gun falling from his nerveless fingers, and there was a splotch of blood on his forehead where the rifle bullet had struck him. At that moment the distant sound of the rifleshot echoed down from the ridge, and McCabe heaved a sigh as he turned and ran around the rear corner of the house. Rosie Dean had not lied about being a good shot.

Moving fast, aware that the shot would have alerted anyone in the house, McCabe reached the back door, which stood ajar, and shouldered his way into a small kitchen. An inner door was wide open and he went forward, his gun ready, emerging into a passage that led to the front of the house. He saw two men standing just inside the front door, peering out through the window beside it.

'I tell you that shot came from the ridge,' one of the men declared, 'and I ain't going out there. I don't get paid enough to take that kind of risk.'

'Conn is out there on watch,' the other replied. 'Get out and check up.'

'What in hell was that shot?' Dave

Thorn appeared on the stairs to the left, descending into McCabe's field of vision. The gambler was holding a gun in his right hand and a large leather case in his left. He looked as if he was planning to make a swift getaway.

'It was a rifleshot, fired a couple of hundred yards out,' one of the men said. 'Conn is on watch, like you told him. You better ask him what's going on. If you're pulling out then it's time we all upped stakes.'

'You're too late.' McCabe eased forward a couple of paces, and three pairs of eyes flickered around to gaze at him. 'Drop your gun, Thorn. You ain't going anywhere, except back to town to face the music. You other two get your hands up before I start shooting holes in you.'

Thorn released his hold on the case and it crashed down the remaining stairs. At the same time the gambler jerked his gunhand around to aim at McCabe. But he was awkwardly positioned, and McCabe squeezed off a shot that drilled through the centre of Thorn's chest. Thorn dropped his gun and clutched at his chest. Then his hand fell to his side and he sprawled down the stairs on his face.

The two men joined the action instinctively, pulling their guns and moving apart as they centred upon McCabe, who moved fast, stepping to the right and dropping to one knee. The man on the right was fast, and a bullet punched through the spot where McCabe's head had been a split second before. McCabe fired, the foresight of his gun lifting slightly as the weapon jerked out its message of death. The bullet took the man in the throat and sent him pitching against his companion, who was in the act of firing. But his aim was thrown off as the gun exploded raucously, and his bullet thudded harmlessly into the wooden floor, throwing up splinters beside McCabe.

Gunsmoke speared across the space between McCabe and the front door.

He fired again, aiming for a shoulder, and the man was slammed backwards against the door by the impact of the powerful slug. He slid down to the floor and lay still as the gun-echoes faded.

McCabe straightened, breathing stertorously, surprised that he had not been touched by the shots directed at him. He checked all three men, finding Thorn and one of the others dead and the third dying.

Reloading his sixgun, McCabe stepped out to the porch. The sound of rapid hooves pounding the sun-baked ground came to his ears as he emerged from the house, the drumming sound chasing out the fading echoes of the shooting. Surprised, he looked around quickly to see two riders coming fast into the yard, followed by another several yards behind.

With a start of cold realization, McCabe recognized the foremost rider as Sam Gotch. There was no mistaking the big outlaw and his scarred face.

Gotch was waving a rifle in the air, shouting as he came.

Fighting down his surprise, McCabe triggered his sixgun, snapping a shot at Gotch. The outlaw was not expecting trouble and the bullet took him by surprise. It thudded into his right shoulder and he lost his grip on his rifle and immediately whirled his horse around to ride out. McCabe fired again, his teeth bared. He wanted Gotch down in the dust. His bullet hit the fleeing outlaw in the centre of the back, shattering the spine, and Gotch yelled thinly in agony as he pitched sideways and fell out of his saddle One foot caught in a stirrup and he was dragged out of the yard by the spooked horse.

McCabe leaned back against the front wall of the house and narrowed his eyes. The second outlaw was lifting a sixgun and the weapon began hammering. Bullets slammed into the wall of the house, drilling through the sun-warped boards very close to McCabe, who dropped to his knees and drew a quick bead on the outlaw.

The rider was hunched over in his saddle to minimize his target area, and McCabe aimed off slightly, allowing for the outlaw's movement. As he fired, a bullet from the third man, coming up swiftly, hit McCabe in the chest with the force of a kicking mule. McCabe, in the act of rising, went crashing backwards. He saw his target pitch out of the saddle and tried to aim at the third rider, but his Colt suddenly seemed as heavy as a cannon and dragged itself out of his hand. As it thudded on the boards of the porch McCabe saw the third rider fall sideways out of his saddle and knew that Rosie had saved him again. Then his sight failed and he plunged into dark silence . . .

Coming back to consciousness was like crawling out of an open grave. McCabe was aware of pain in his chest, and, lifting a hand to the area, he was surprised to find that he was tightly bandaged. He opened his eyes, blinked to focus them, and realized he was lying on a bed in a small room. The setting sun was cutting in at one corner of the window, and he guessed the evening was well advanced.

Voices attracted his attention and he looked around to see Rosie and Frank Holbrooke standing by the door. Rosie was talking furiously.

'You're not moving him out of here, Holbrooke,' she was saying. 'He stays until he's fit enough to walk out on his own two legs. He's done a lot for me and I'm gonna repay him.'

'I got another job for him,' Holbrooke said harshly, 'now he's finished this one.'

'He's not fit to feed a calf let alone go out man-hunting. You get out of here, mister. I'll tell him to report to you when he feels well enough.'

'How about some peace so I can rest up?' McCabe demanded.

'How you feeling, feller?' Holbrooke

grinned, turning to the bed. 'You had me worried some, Cole. I came out from town with a bunch of men to give you a hand to wind up the case and found it was all settled.'

'I guess I'll make it.' McCabe grunted as pain lanced through his shoulder.

'The doc said you would,' Rosie told him. 'But you got to rest up and give yourself time to heal.'

'I'll surely do that.' McCabe looked Holbrooke in the eyes with steady gaze. 'When I do get on my feet I figure to change my way of life. You're gonna need someone you can trust to help you run this place, Rosie, and I always did fancy myself as a rangehand.'

'So that's the way the wind blows, huh?' Holbrooke nodded slowly. 'I got to be on my way now, but I'll be back in Hickory in about three weeks. We'll talk then, Cole. I allus said you could quit when you felt like it, and you sure made me happy during our association.'

'I feel like quitting now,' McCabe said quietly, his eyes narrowing as he considered his recent past. 'It's been a long road, but every trail has an ending.'

He closed his eyes and drifted into a pain-racked sleep, relieved that a decision had evolved as a natural culmination of events, aware that he had reached a big milestone in his life and certain that he had made the right decision. By the time he recovered from his wound the past would be where it belonged and the future, whatever transpired, would be awaiting him with open arms. He could ask for no more.

THE END

DEATH MARCH IN MONTANA

Bill Foord

Held under armed guard in a Union prison camp, Captain Pat Quaid learns that the beautiful wife of the sadistic commandant wants her husband killed. She engineers the escape of Quaid and his young friend Billy Childs in exchange for Quaid's promise to turn hired gunman. He has reasons enough to carry out the promise, but he's never shot a man in cold blood. Can he do it for revenge, hatred or love?

A LAND TO DIE FOR

Tyler Hatch

There were two big ranches in the valley: Box T and Flag. Ben Tanner's Box T was the larger and he ran things his way. Wes Flag seemed content to play second fiddle to Tanner — until he married Shirley. But the trouble hit the valley and soon everyone was involved. Now it was all down to Tanner's loyal ramrod, Jesse McCord. He had to face some tough decisions if he was to bring peace to the troubled range — and come out alive.

THE SAN PEDRO RING

Elliot Conway

US Marshal Luther Killeen is working undercover as a Texan pistolero in Tucson to find proof that the San Pedro Ring, an Arizona trading and freighting business concern, is supplying arms to the bronco Apache in the territory. But the fat is truly in the fire when his real identity is discovered. Clelland Singer, the ruthless boss of the Ring, hires a professional killer, part-Sioux Louis Merlain, to hunt down Luther. Now it is a case of kill or be killed.